Heather Hughes-Calero
THE SEDONA TRILOGY
Book One
Through the Crystal

Presented with love . . . in SUGMAD.

COASTLINE PUBLISHING COMPANY
Post Office Box 223062
Carmel, California 93922
1985

THE SEDONA TRILOGY

Book One *Through the Crystal*
by Heather Hughes-Calero

COASTLINE PUBLISHING COMPANY
Post Office Box 223062
Carmel, California 93922

Cover design by Lois Stanfield.

Library of Congress Catalog No.: 85-89056.
ISBN: 0-932927-00-9

*To Hank, my special friend and
partner in life.*

Forthcoming Titles. . . .
by Heather Hughes-Calero

THE SEDONA TRILOGY:

Book Two
Doorways Between the Worlds

THE SEDONA TRILOGY:

Book Three
Land of Nome

For further information write:

COASTLINE PUBLISHING COMPANY
Post Office Box 223062
Carmel, California 93922

CHAPTER 1

Deetra had heard the Askans were to attend the Awakening Day Centennial; that once every hundred years they made themselves visible to the world, but she couldn't believe it. In all her youth she had heard nothing but frightful stories about them; sometimes referred to as the "rock people" who had hearts of stone and who lived invisibly within the giant crimson cliffs. Some also said the red-rock mountains were peculiarly shaped like bells and temples and faces because the Askans thought them up that way. It was said that the whole world would change or even disappear if the Askan wished it. To Deetra this was the point which spurred her on. Only one person in her village was old enough to remember the last Awakening Day Ceremony.

★ ★ ★

The old man was said to be mute to conceal the many things he knew. He sat alone near Tower Rock with an empty wooden bowl on his lap. Occasionally a villager passed by depositing a bit of food or gently placing a gift on his lap. No one dared to ask him a question, and Deetra was a girl among other girls supposed to work the fields and not question an ancient mystery. She did not know why she was compelled to question. The other villagers seemed content with the legends they passed among themselves, not sure the Askans actually existed, but Deetra found herself discontented, wanting to know more.

The ritual of caring for the old man satisfied the others. They fed him, clothed him, kept his hut neat, did everything they could to make him comfortable and found that that was enough for them. But to Deetra there was a voice to the old man's silence about the meaning of the Askans which she knew was most important, understood only by the old man.

Why?

Why was the old man the only one alive who knew the secrets and why was he mute? If Awakening Day, which occurred only once a century, was not remembered by anyone who could speak about it; if the Askans were only legend after all, why have it at all?

"These things are no concern of the village people," her father told her. "Hanta is special. He was chosen a century ago to be the lone rememberer of Awakening Day. He carries the burden of keeping It alive in his heart, unable to speak to us who have not experienced It. He has nothing of the love and companionship we ordinary people have among ourselves. He lives alone and carries the memory, the meaning of our lives upon his shoulders. See sometimes how he bends with the weight of silence?"

Deetra thought about the old man. He was more than a century old, bent and wrinkled like a dried prune. It seemed he could not live much longer. But now another image of the old man came to the girl's mind. Early mornings when he came to his stone seat beneath Tower Rock his back was straight and he walked erect and steady. He sat and was transformed. Deetra had seen him, his continence a flow of light, a magnetic feeling about him, a feeling of love, of peace and equally so of great mystery.

Deetra was disturbed considering this matter, and one day she asked her father, "What if Hanta dies? Is there no one else who remembers the Askans. Would there still be an Awakening Day ceremony?"

"We are not to be concerned about it," her father said. "There has always been a Hanta."

And he would say no more.

"There has always been a Hanta."

How that sentence mystified Deetra.

Who else would it be?

Deetra felt she must get some answers.

Hanta lived alone with a young man, Ian, assigned by the village elders to care for the needs of the old man. Ian hardly ever spoke except when spoken to, answering simple questions for his master's benefactors from the village. When it was the turn of Deetra's family to provide food for the household, Deetra volunteered to take it, hoping to have an opportunity of conversation. But neither Hanta nor Ian were at home and Deetra was forced to leave the food and return to her chores.

But one day when Deetra had maneuvered herself between the adults gathered about the stones of Tower Rock in preparation for Awakening Day ceremonies, she looked up quickly, sensing the Hanta's eyes looking into hers'. She had the peculiar feeling that the Ancient One could see into her and read her every thought. She felt she saw the old man's lips move as if to speak to her or was it a light smile. Whatever, the moment fleeted so quickly, the old man's face again so expressionless that she could not be sure she imagined it. She knew suddenly she was trembling and her head felt as though it was bursting with a humming sound.

★ ★ ★

Until that moment she had been aware of him as Hanta's servant, a young man not much older than herself, simply dressed and rather plain looking and therefore not much interest to her. Hanta was more curious looking

[*3*]

to her, always speechless although appearing to speak, replying to questions by not answering and displaying motion while seemingly absolutely still.

It was on a day that her father had sent her on an errand to the marketplace that she had witnessed a strange occurrence. Ian was the center of it. She saw him standing, leaning against a stone pillar, looking at her while she finished paying for the piece of cloth she was purchasing. She could feel his eyes and she turned toward him, slipping her purse back into the pocket beneath her apron. She had never noticed how strong and muscular he was but the casual way he stood now seemed to exemplify his build.

He smiled and reached into his pocket, motioning to her with his free hand.

Deetra studied the firm, handsome features of the young man's face. It was as though she had never really seen him. For an instant she thought she saw Hanta standing next to him, but just as suddenly the image was gone.

The young man approached, the palm of his right hand open and extended toward her. On it was something shiney, a pebble of sorts.

"There is more to the ceremonies than legend would tell," he said suddenly.

"What do you mean?"

She had moved toward him and stopped abruptly as a passerby walked between them and curiously looked back over their shoulder. She could hear the faint sound of bees humming and wondered at the sound.

"Perhaps you would like to learn more?" he asked.

Ian's hand was no longer extended and the pebble he held was nowhere in sight.

"Perhaps."

"It's an experience on many levels," he said calmly.

She stared at him astonished. His face had a strange expression.

"You know I am right," he continued patiently, "there is no need for you to pretend."

She did not know what to say. She had been curious, had indulged herself for many hours privately wondering the purpose and depth of the great day to come.

He was looking into her calmly and for a moment she had the same strange sensation that she had felt when she had met the eyes of the Ancient One.

Ian was seeing into her mind.

He also knew things she didn't know.

She was shocked and dismissed the idea immediately.

"I have to go!" She was anxious and the ring of her words echoed.

"It's all right to know more," he said. "The true meaning of Awakening Day will be revealed to those who sincerely want to know."

Ian smiled, and Deetra saw that there was a keen gentleness in his face.

"If you wish to know more and prepare yourself I will meet with you again."

"Where?"

"I will send a message," he said.

Then he was gone. The marketplace suddenly became very busy. She caught a last glimpse of Ian moving away from her among the people. She stood there seemingly alone. The sound of bees she had heard earlier seemed to hum all about her. She remained still momentarily unable to think of anything else.

Some time passed. It rained a great deal and Deetra remained indoors helping her mother with sewing and cleaning. Occasionally she thought of Ian and Hanta but her images of them seemed less mysterious and casual family preparations for the Awakening Day ceremonies made the event to come seem more like legend than ever before.

On the next marketing day something occured to renew her suspicion that Ian was not quite an ordinary person.

The people were gathered along the merchant's stalls bargaining, and chattering about the festivity that was still some months away. The sun was bright and in the clear sky an outline of the moon was still visible.

Suddenly there was commotion. A small band of men were leading someone through the marketplace. They were leading Hanta. Ian was directly behind him.

The procession stopped.

Deetra watched as a village Elder came toward her and held out his hand. On it was the shiney clear glass pebble like the one Ian had once outstretched to her.

"Take it my child," the Elder said.

Deetra's eyes met Ian. He nodded as if to approve.

"Take it my child," the Elder said again. "You will be given instructions at a later time."

Deetra lifted the pebble from the Elder's hand, watching as the Elder moved away and rejoined the small procession as it slowly left the marketplace. All about her was the subtle, almost imperceptible hum of bees.

★   ★   ★

Deetra tucked the pebble into the pocket beneath her apron and left the marketplace. She wanted to be somewhere alone; to examine the pebble and to think over what had happened. Instinctively she knew her curiosity was drawing peculiar events toward her. It was a lesson she had learned well as a young child. Whenever she wondered about anything intently, her wish was granted. Only now she was only half-sure that she really wanted answers. A feeling within cautioned her.

Beneath the large oak tree in the meadow between the mountains near her home she found solace. She drew the pebble from beneath her apron and held it up to the light. Yellow rays of sunlight passed through it. It was glass.

No.

It was crystal. She remembered long ago seeing such a crystal. It had been her grandfathers'. As a small girl she had seen him on occasions looking dreamily into it. He had said that it was his window to view the world. He had it the night he died and Deetra had supposed it had been buried with him. Now, gazing at the curious stone, Deetra recalled how she had loved her grandfather; his gentleness; his reverence for all of life, and she remembered too her mother once telling her that grandfather personally tended to the needs of Hanta.

Did Hanta give him the crystal?

The elder who handed her the crystal at the marketplace. Did he too have a crystal?

Deetra's mind exploded with question. The unusual sound of humming bees filled her with a light feeling in mind and body. She felt as if living a dream—omnipresent, dimension within dimension and the softness of color and sound enhanced it.

"And now I will tell you about the crystal," the voice said.

Ian stood above her, smiling, motioning for her to rise.

She stood up, unsure if she were dreaming, extending the crystal between them.

"The crystal is to help you see between the worlds— the inner as well as the outer and all the worlds inbetween. But that will take time because the worlds are like planes or levels of consciousness, one overlapping the other—separate but truly ONE."

Tiny flecks of light danced about them as Ian spoke and then she couldn't hear him anymore. Now it wasn't Ian who stood before her but Hanta and he was old one moment and young the next. And then it wasn't Hanta at all but herself—herself, Hanta and Ian all ONE. She wasn't sure where she began and the others left off. They were all one person, one entity yet separate, humming particles of light.

Ian was gone.

Hanta was gone.

She was alone, as herself alone.

She did not dare to look at the crystal pebble again. Carefully, she tucked it beneath her apron and hurried for home.

Deetra's pace slowed as she neared her home. She was alone, and yet not altogether. The memory of her meeting with Ian silhouetted the huge landscape, the gigantic red mountains that ruled over her life slid past her into the deep shadows to the west, the haunting rock sentinels growing taller as they grew darker and sharper in outline against the brilliant luminosity of the sky.

Deetra trembled as she looked up at them. They had always seemed dark and forbidding before, protective as well, a matter of fact. Only now it rushed in to her thoughts that somehow her destiny was with them and her life as a child working and playing in the fields was about to change. She stopped walking and stared at them. They grew taller and taller, dark shapes reaching great lengths into infinity, the light behind them unfolding startling colors from pale yellows to stark incredible white. It seemed to her that she was looking into the heart of the light and it was enveloping her.

She covered her face with her hands and squeezed her eyes shut to block out the piercing light, but she could still see it beneath her eyelids.

The crystal was within her in some way, and yet, at the same time, outside her, encompassing everything which existed.

She encompassed all that existed!

She was everything and all things were her.

Her father was shaking her.

"Deetra, Deetra!" he was calling, his expression filled with anxiety. "What is it Deetra?"

Her vision disappeared and she was left a shaken and trembling little girl in the semi-darkness, her father's strong hands upon her shoulders, his concerned face studying her.

Still trembling, she looked about her. The light was gone and the sky was rapidly growing dark. The mountains appeared very ordinary and were gradually fading from sight, a late flying formation of birds flew above them. Friendly smoke from home fires was rising beyond the meadow.

★　★　★

Nearly a month passed without further incident. The afternoon in the meadow with Ian now seemed as though a dream and Deetra would have left it at that except for the contents of a pouch she now wore about her waist. In it was the crystal. Frequently when alone she took it out and examined it. The light shined through it as before but nothing else. Nothing happened. She did not look for Ian nor did she ask about him. Yet she could not forget. The crystal reminded her.

Then one day the Elders called a meeting of the community to discuss final preparations for Awakening Day.

There was whispering and grumbling from the men

who were gathered. It was not convenient to leave their work, but an order from the Elders could not be ignored.

Deetra joined the others and hurried through the fields to the gathering place.

Village gatherings were usually held at the base of Bell Rock, a bell-shaped mountain which towered above the settlement. At the base was a smaller rock structure which served as a platform, flanked on either side by long, narrow stone benches. To the East and West the jagged red sandstone cliffs formed a perfect amplitheatre.

While the people were arriving the Elders sat in dignified silence along the benches, and when everyone was present and the expectant chattering had died down, their chief spokesman climbed atop the platform. His name was Sarpent.

"Awakening Day is but a moon away," said Sarpent. "We must finish preparations. There is much that must yet be accomplished."

"Moonwalk must be prepared. Hanta will retreat there beginning the new moon and will remain until the ceremony is complete. No one is to go near the area except those agreed upon by this council. Until the height of the full moon Moonwalk is forbidden ground."

Sarpent paused, waiting for the sudden murmur in the gathering to quiet. Although seldom did anyone from the village climb to the far reaches of Moonwalk, it was the first time a villager had ever been forbidden to go there.

"Listen carefully," Sarpent's voice rose above the gathering. "Instructions I am about to give come from Hanta, the Silent One."

The gathering moved uneasily and fell silent again.

"Hanta has been silent for nearly one hundred years. On Awakening Day he will have fulfilled the great task given him by the Askan. Hanta's silence has been for our freedom to experience this great day. However, there are three laws:

"One . . . Moonwalk is forbidden ground until that morning of the full moon when all will gather on the foundation.

"Two . . . The harvest must be completed by dawn on Awakening Day.

"Three . . . Listen carefully. This is the most difficult. Beginning the new moon morning, two days hence, every villager will maintain *silence*."

Sarpent paused again.

A rush of chattering shot through the gathering, gradually quieting again.

"The great truth of Awakening Day will be worth the effort. The truth is not myth as many have supposed. This is your lifetime opportunity. No one in the village is to speak for any reason from the new moon until the ceremony is complete."

No one in the gathering stirred. Sarpent waved his hands in conclusion and stepped down from the platform.

A kind of movement went through the crowd that Deetra had seen in a wheat field on a windy day. The amplitheatre did not seem to be covered with individuals but with a kind of composite being that reached, signed and moved as one. Deetra, seeing it, felt herself separate and apart.

As she turned away, Ian was there next to her.

"And now the experience unfolds," he said, smiling slightly.

Deetra did not answer. A sudden memory of her experience with the crystal rushed at her. Ian was not a vision now. She could see how real he was, could touch him if she wished and she wanted to but did not dare.

"It is only the beginning," Ian said again, "or the end, whichever you want it to be."

The people were disbanding quickly and the murmuring that was all about was now fading in the distance. In the growing quiet a new sound was prevading. It was subtle yet distinct, a hum of sorts. Deetra had heard it before.

"I want to know . . ." Deetra said, not wanting to complete her thought aloud.

"That's why I've come."

Ian's keen blue eyes held hers'. The impulse to touch him rose in her again and embarrassed she stepped back.

Ian smiled.

He knew.

"I'm as real as you. My task until now has been different than yours', that's all."

"What do you mean?" she asked impatiently.

"Now you are beginning to believe in the importance of Awakening Day. Before you didn't."

"Everyone is feeling something," she said. "Everyone. How can the Elders expect a whole community to maintain silence?"

"What will be, will be. Some won't, but the majority . . the majority recognize the opportunity. They know something is to happen that will not happen again in their lifetime. They know that Hanta is not a myth, nor that he is just another old man. And the proof of what will be will come as he leaves for the mountain at the new moon."

Ian hesitated, looking deeply into her. "And that is why I'm here with you now."

"Is Hanta to die?" she asked, avoiding the question she wanted to ask.

"That is his choice. He may choose to remain as the Ancient One; to live out another century in his role, or he may pass the rod of power to another."

Deetra's mind reeled with question. Everything within her was screaming in confusion. All the simplicity of life as she had known it was transforming. Now she felt she was certain of nothing at all. She was no longer just a young girl with simple responsibilities. There was Hanta, Ian, the crystal . . . and all of the mystery and wonder of Awakening Day. Suddenly life was becoming dreamlike. Perhaps she would awaken to find herself lying in bed, marvelling at a great story.

Ian's voice interrupted. "You were given the crystal because you can be made ready to assist Hanta in His work."

"Why me?"

"You earned it. We have all lived many lifetimes. We evolved through the mineral, vegetable and animal worlds. Many of us have been human for many, many lives. Some of us have learned our lessons more completely than others. Those who reach a certain stage in their spiritual development are offered an opportunity to work with the Ancient One. In this and every time the Ancient One's name is Hanta, which means the One who remembers and guides."

"What of the crystal?"

"All questions are answered in their own time," Ian said gently. "To tell you everything now would be impossible. If you choose, I will take you to Hanta who will open you to the wonders of all life. If you choose not to, the crystal will gradually become a mere pebble. You will eventually tire of it and toss it away."

Deetra again thought of her grandfather; how she had seen him lovingly gaze at the crystal; how she had heard he was an attendant to Hanta. Her mother had said he had been chosen.

"I will go with you," she said to Ian.

Ian smiled warmly. "I was hoping you would."

[*13*]

"When?"

"At the dawn of the new moon you will meet me at Tower Rock. Be seated on Hanta's stone bench and wait for me there."

Deetra watched as Ian turned and walked away, moving gracefully and strong, disappearing behind the rock at the north entrance of the amplitheatre. There was no point in staying any longer. She hurried out of the area and went directly home.

While the rest of the village was anticipating the arrival of Awakening Day and the long silence which was to begin at the new moon, Deetra was uneasy and intrigued by what awaited her.

When she had returned home she called her family together and told them in sequence as best she could of the crystal, of Hanta and Ian and what she knew of her role in Awakening Day preparations. Although concerned, her mother and father accepted her fate as they had accepted grandfathers. It was, they knew, a blessing to the individual, to the family and to the community. Their daughter must not be denied this great opportunity.

Later that afternoon Deetra's father came to her as he had done whenever he had felt her in a difficult situation. It was uncanny how he always knew, always there when she needed the comfort of being a little girl again. She nestled in his arms and wept lightly, not because she was frightened but because the uncertainty of growing and learning without those she knew and loved at her side.

"My daughter," her father said gently. "There are things I must tell you, things my father, your grandfather passed on to me."

Deetra straightened herself, her eyes meeting her father's tender gaze.

"Long ago the people of this village made a pledge. The pledge was not a simple one and yet it was—to serve

[*14*]

the Great One as a channel for the Divine Force." He hesitated seeing the question on her face. "Yes, even though your name was not Deetra in the ancient days when the pledge was made, you were there in another body in that other time as one who made the pledge. We all were. We bonded ourselves to a responsibility.

"Awakening Day is a realization of that responsibility for some. Once every hundred years the people of the village prepare. Many think the event only to be a tradition and do not take it seriously. They see Hanta as nothing more than an old man. The Laws, the silence imposed by the Elders is seen as a game and a challenge. Some will realize its meaning as time goes on; others will not. It does not matter. Those who do not realize its meaning now will realize it another time, another century, another Awakening Day. There is no rush for anyone. When realization comes to the individual, it comes; and the coming of it begins with curiosity and question—because curiosity and question are a sign that inwardly the person already knows. He or she need only be conscious of the knowing." He paused, looking at Deetra. "That is why my daughter, you have been chosen. Your questions are leading you to the answers."

Deetra was longing to ask about her grandfather, but it came to her that her father knew what her grandfather had known and the realization of it astonished her. He had never spoken of these things before now.

Her father reached in the cloth pouch that was belted about his waist and withdrew a crystal. Although it was the same as her own, it appeared very tiny in his large hand.

"Do not be afraid to use your crystal," he said.

"But how do I use it father?"

"You will learn. It is not for me to teach you. You are in the loving hands of the Hanta. But I can tell you this.

Whenever you feel discouraged you may use the crystal to call on me for encouragement. You are not my daughter by accident, but by bond. Do you understand?"

Deetra nodded, although not certain that she did.

"Now my daughter we must return to the others. The Elders will be wanting to see us." Taking Deetra by the hand, they arose and walked slowly back to the house.

★ ★ ★

For the next two days the community prepared for the new moon and how they would handle the long silence ahead. The Elders made their rounds to each home, discussing each family's individual circumstances. Women with small children could converse in low voice whenever necessary. Although whispering was discouraged, this manner of conversing could be used in urgent matters. It was suggested however, that hand and other silent signals be set up for most urgent situations and that for the most part communication could be learned telepathically. A simple exercise was given to each member of the community to ensure inner and outer peace in the trial ahead. These were the instructions:

To sit quietly for one-half hour each morning thinking only of Hanta and the meaning of Awakening Day. At the end of that period of time, each was to spend an additional few moments contemplating what needed to be accomplished that day. If it was working-hand-in-hand with someone, they were to visualize the image of Hanta superimposed over the image of their co-worker.

It was told to all that the image of Hanta would counteract any difficulty, and that during this long period of quiet, each was to focus their attention within, listening for the voice of silence.

That was all.

CHAPTER 2

Deetra hurried through the village. The small hut-like houses were already alive with activity. Some were carrying wood inside; others were leaving to work in the fields and still others were standing in the open, looking about in uncomfortable anticipation. Many saw her as she moved up the narrow street but no one said a word. It was the dawn of the new moon and the law of silence was in effect.

Hurriedly, she passed house after house, her small bundle of personal belongings bouncing uncomfortably strapped to her back. She cut through the meadow. The lone oak where she once sat to study her crystal seemed to nod at her as she passed. She dared not think of it now, nor did she acknowledge the subtle rise of a humming sound which seemed to follow her, nor the stillness of her heart which seemed not to beat at all. Her course was steady and quick and at last when she arrived at Tower Rock she felt as if she were barely breathing. The hum she had heard was not outside her now, but inside as though she was a part of it, and it her.

She was not alone.

Hanta's bench beneath Tower Rock held two boys slightly younger than herself. She recognized them and nodded without speaking. It was Curtser the miller's son and Rian the village orphan. They seemed surprised as she but quickly caught themselves and moved down on the bench to make room for her. She took her seat.

They waited.

Deetra reflected on the two boys next to her and she sensed they thought of her as well. Curtser had a reputation for inventiveness and courage. He had saved a woman's life when she fell into the path of his father's windmill by jamming the apparatus with a clump of hay, and then used the incident as a means for discovering a breaking device for the mill. Little was known about Rian. His parents abandoned him at birth, leaving him on the very bench where they were sitting now. One of the Elders found him and gave him a home. Later he worked in the fields and lived with a different villager with each new moon. That was all Deetra knew of the boy. She had never heard anything good or bad about him. He was hardworking but quiet and reserved and no one spent their time speaking of him.

Deetra wondered if the boys had a crystal; if Ian had visited with them as well as she, and if they too were to journey to Moonwalk and Hanta.

The air was completely still. The two boys next to Deetra had not moved, nor had she. They sat like three stone statues, wondering at the stillness. There was not a bird or insect or any other form of life seemingly alive at that moment. It was as though the moment was a dream, heightening as the rising sun rubbed against their faces, blinding their distant vision with an array of colorful lights.

It seemed they had waited a very long time and then suddenly Ian was there, standing before them. His expression was somber but kind and his manner gentle.

"Are you ready?" Ian asked.

[*18*]

Deetra nodded and noted that the two boys did so as well.

"Then follow me," Ian said, "and stay close together. We have a long journey and little time for rest along the way."

Deetra was first to her feet. Ian noted her and motioned to the others that they be on their way.

★ ★ ★

Their course was set due north, behind Tower Rock to the narrow trail which rose into the mountains and disappeared into the dark terrain. It was the path to Moonwalk but not the usual one. The way to Moonwalk which Deetra had once travelled was a wide road which began near her father's house at the far end of the village. The way they were travelling now held no memory for her. She wondered if Hanta had come this way. She could not imagine the steps of the Ancient One on so difficult a path. All about them was jagged terrain, dotted with catsclaw and chapparal. The way was steep, yet the path itself was clear of any obstacles and to her surprise they seemed to cover a great distance in a short period of time.

Ian stopped and turned to the others. "We will rest here," he said, motioning to a large flat rock beneath a clump of pine trees.

It was the first time that Deetra had looked back. Young Rian was a matter of a few feet behind, puffing slightly as he came to join them on the rock. But Curtser was no where in sight. She looked to Ian who as she seemed not to be disturbed by the climb at all.

"We will wait for him," Ian said.

In the distance a small, tired figure was seen gradually ascending. As the figure grew closer, it grew larger until they could see it was indeed Curtser catching up with them. When at last he joined them to rest on the rock, Ian spoke in the most astonishing way.

[*19*]

"When we began," he said firmly, "I instructed all of you to stay close." there was a reason for these instructions. Now perhaps you are ready to understand.

"This is not my first journey along this path. I know it well and I am conditioned to it. That is why I am not in the least fatigued." Ian looked at the faces of his companions before continuing: "Deetra has never travelled this path before but she stayed close; her steps followed my steps and as you will see she is not fatigued."

Astonished, Deetra eyes met Ian.

"The three of you have already begun to realize a great truth. Those closest to the source are closest to IT. I am a channel as you will be. Hanta is the greatest living channel of all. In his presence you will notice me little because his Being is closest to the source.

"The example we just experienced should help you understand. As our little band straggled, the energy dissipated. Rian was slightly more tired than Deetra, and Curtser who was in little step with us at all found the climb extremely difficult. It is important that the attention of each of you be purely focused on the task at hand. The task, in this case a physical task, is the tool to hold that attention. But there are other tasks than physical ones, and you will come to know and understand these in another way. Now," Ian said rising, "we must be on our way."

This time the little band stuck closely together. Curtser who had previously tailed the group now moved easily just inches behind Ian, and Deetra and Rian had to move more quickly in order to hold a parallel place along the path. It wasn't until past mid-day when they stopped again. There was a fork in the road; one which continued to climb into the mountain and the other which took a level wind to the right.

Ian turned and surveyed his charges. All eyes were upon him as if waiting for his next move. He smiled. "I can see that the lesson has been learned. None of you appear to require rest, however we'll stay here a bit. You may move about and do as you wish."

Ian sat comfortably, leaning against a Pinon tree, his legs stretched in front of him and closed his eyes. Curtser and Rian crossed the path together and sat down on a rock which overlooked the valley below. Deetra thought about joining them but preferred a little time to herself. Instead she unstrapped the napsack from her back and set out to walk along the level path just to the right ahead of them.

As she had expected the trail was flat, gently winding next to the traversing slope. There was a lightness to her steps and a feeling of joy. A soft breeze tickled her cheeks. She marvelled at the scenic beauty about her; at the crystal-clear air, so clear that it glittered and sparkled about her. The foliage was alive, dancing to it. The rock about her was alive and so was the brilliant blue sky above and the red soil beneath her feet. She began to hum a tune, a tune she had heard on occasion. It was the crystal's tune, the mysterious hum that had filled her when she had first met Hanta and Ian; the tune that had rushed within her as she had hurried to meet him at Tower Rock earlier. The crystal was in her pouch tied about her waist and she did not reach for it. It was there, she knew, but it was also everywhere. Perhaps she was not outside the crystal or it not outside her. Perhaps she was within it. What was to come? In her wonderment, she stopped, and as she did so she saw that she was not alone.

Just ahead, standing on a precipice stood the strong but ancient figure of Hanta. She could not see the full of his face. His attention seemed held by the vast reaches of space. It was as though he were deep in thought and unaware that she was present.

Deetra did not move. Her mind raced in various directions, wondering at what to do—to quickly return to the others or to stay. She realized that Hanta was no ordinary being. Although he had not acknowledged her with his eyes nor said a word, he was talking to her through the silence.

"Come here my child," he was saying. "We have much to share. You have entered the crystal; the world between the worlds and it is here that I can teach you all."

The voice was not a voice and yet it was. Deetra was drawn to it and comforted. To her surprise she realized she was not afraid. Her thoughts quieted and she no longer wished to run away or to call out to her companions. Something was happening. She was not in the presence of a stranger but someone she knew well; someone she trusted and with whom she was completely comfortable.

Hanta turned to her, a knowing smile motioned her to him. A great feeling of love passed from him to her and it joined them together. She was now on the precipice next to him aware of the greatest joy she had ever known. About them the world sparkled and glittered like a prism. Light refractions—reflections reflecting reflections and there was a melody to the moment. The hum she had heard earlier was transformed into music but none like she had ever heard. It was music and the hum together; sounds of the glittering world. She did not know how she knew it, but she knew. Here between the worlds in another plane of being she was experiencing the light and sound of a divine source. She knew it to be the essence of all life—the creator and the destroyer, dual on one hand and purely positive on the other. They were both, yet one as she and Hanta were two but one. All about them was proof of this divine substance. The physical world was part of it, but also merely an outer shell, as her own body was the essence within. The outer shell was not the illusion, but rather the limited consciousness that that was all there was.

In the distance, Deetra heard a voice calling her. Gradually it drew her attention and the image of Hanta and the world between the worlds faded.

"Deetra . . . Deetra . . . You had better hurry," the voice called. It was Rian's voice. He rushed to her on the ledge, then took a step back, studying her. His eyes reflected the beauty of what she had experienced. He knew. And as she went with him to rejoin the others, she felt very happy at having found a friend.

★ ★ ★

As one comes in from the dazzling light only to find themselves blinded by the dim, Deetra returned to her companions feeling somewhat vague about what had happened. She kept her memory of the incident to herself. If Ian suspected anything he didn't say and Curtser showed no interest. Rian was her constant reminder. Whenever a moment alone permitted, Rian questioned her.

"What did you see in the light?"

"Did Hanta speak to you?"

"Did he speak to you about the crystal?"

"How far did he take you into the other world?"

"Did he tell you of what is to come?"

The questions seemed endless. Finally Deetra knew she would have to say something, so she asked Rian how the Ancient One had chosen him.

Rian knew that Deetra had shifted the subject to himself but he was pleased to have her attention all the same. "Hanta first visited me when I was working the miller's fields," he said. "It was then that I was given the crystal."

Deetra was astonished. "You mean Hanta gave you the crystal himself?"

"Yes."

"In what way?" Deetra was extremely interested now.

"That I can't tell you," the boy said, turning away.

He had asked for it. He had begun by asking her questions about things she wasn't able to talk about, and now he was the questioned.

Deetra pulled back. She understood. Yet one more question. "Isn't the music strangely lovely?" she asked, catching the quick turn of his head. His eyes sparkled momentarily before he turned away again.

He knew.

Deetra pondered the recognition in Rian's eyes. Curtser had shown no interest in Deetra, nor Rian. He had stayed close only to Ian since the incident early in their journey. It was as if he was glued to the older boy; cared or experienced nothing except following Ian's footsteps. Surely that could not be true however. He was the miller's son. Was he with Rian when Hanta gave him the crystal? Or did Ian meet with him as he had done with her? Had Curtser ever experienced a meeting with Hanta? Suddenly she had to know.

She waited until the right moment when the little band had once again separated for a rest period. Curtser, who was watching to see if Ian was to settle in a particular spot, saw her coming. He eyed the older girl suspiciously.

"I suppose we're almost there," the girl said easily, sitting on the ground next to him.

"What makes you say that?"

"It feels that way, don't you think?"

"No." He looked away to where Ian was sitting with his eyes closed.

"You're very close to him, aren't you?" she asked, trying again to lead Curtser into conversation.

He flashed her a hard look, then turned away.

"I suppose I am curious," she said softly, "as to how each of us came on this journey."

"How do you think?" the boy snapped.

"Perhaps the same, but differently."

There was a long silence and Deetra wished that she

hadn't approached the subject.

Curtser looked at her; his expression softened. "I was told to come."

Something in the boy's tone embarrassed Deetra and she rose to her feet.

"I'm sorry," the boy said. "I didn't mean to be rude. I'm here because my father asked Ian to take me. I'm told there's something in me that's lacking and I'm here to find out what it is. Like Rian there," he pointed to the younger boy who was watching them some distance away.

"Let's move on," Ian called. Relieved, Deetra hurried over the dry brush and rock, scrambling for her knapsack next to the trail. Ian's eyes caught hers, then looked away. The look had cautioned her and she knew now to keep to herself.

★ ★ ★

The last part of the journey was the most difficult. The trail was dusty and frought with obstacles. A recent rock slide made it necessary for them to detour through the thick shrubbery. Following in Ian's footsteps was impossible now. As he hurried his way in the lead the thorny catsclaw seemed not to touch him, but it grabbed at Deetra's clothes and scratched her skin. Both Rian and Curtser were behind her, struggling to keep up. It seemed endless. The way was no longer visible. Gusts of wind twisted and swirled, blinding them. Deetra recalled village tales of travellers becoming lost in mountain sandstorms. As a child she was often cautioned never to wander into the mountains alone, but she was not alone now. Behind her the two boys stood with covered faces waiting for a sign as to which way to go. She thought of Ian, how easily he seemed to move through the thorny bush. Did he not realize that they were no longer following him? She would have liked to sit and rest and think but the bush rose like daggers from their feet to their heads and they could not move. If only the wind would cease; if she could see which way to go. Uncertain, she remained motionless, listening as if to the wind. It seemed to be a clue. A sound vaguely familiar seemed to draw her within. It was the crystal's sound and Ian—as One. Listening, she called to the boys to lock hands with her. There was a warmth, a feeling of comfort, appreciation and recognition in Rian's hand, and as she listened again, the sound within the wind seemed to have a direction to it. With her thoughts calling out to Ian, she led her companions toward it, off to the right next to the mountain and ducked into a cave.

They brushed themselves off and looked about. The cave was empty but deep and roomy with a place built up for a fire in the center. It was obvious from the coals that someone had recently spent the night there. The red sand floor held traces of footprints, and there was a sign—a large circle drawn on the wall, with a black dot and a long narrow line leading out of it.

"I have seen that symbol before," Rian said.

"Where?"

Rian was quiet and thoughtful for a moment. "On the speaker's platform at Bell Rock."

Deetra turned to Rian, studying the boy's face, remembering she had heard that he was reared by Sarpent the Elder.

As an infant Sarpent would leave me on the platform for safe keeping while he and the other Elders worked in contemplation. I recall tracing the image of it with my fingers over and over again as I waited."

"What does it mean?"

"I don't know, or remember," the boy said thoughtfully.

"You never asked?"

"When I was old enough to realize it had meaning, I no longer lived with Sarpent. My days were filled with other things and I no longer thought of it."

Deetra recalled an image of Sarpent, his stern, forbidding features and she knew that if she had been Rian, she never would have asked either.

Suddenly Rian spun around. "Where's Curtser?"

Deetra too looked about the cave. Together they called him.

Curtser reappeared, coming from the dark depth of the cave, and hurrying toward them. "I have found a passage," he said.

"A passage?" Rian asked. "That's it. The line leading out of the circle is the passage out of the cave."

"Are you sure?" Deetra asked. "You said you didn't know the meaning of the symbol."

"Well I wasn't sure if I didn't remember or if I didn't know. It was such a long time ago."

"And now you remember?"

"Yes."

"What symbol?" Curtser asked.

Deetra pointed it out to him on the wall.

"That's it, all right," Curtser said. "This cave is the circle. Look at it . . . a perfect circle. The dot is the opening or doorway, and the line is the passage out of it."

"But what does it mean?" Deetra asked, thinking aloud.

"It's the symbol from the Elder's platform," Rian said.

"Then we must follow it," Curtser said.

"Wait," said Deetra, "what of Ian?"

The three fell silent. They had been following Ian when nature and the elements trapped them.

"How did you know this cave was here?" Curtser asked Deetra.

"I didn't. I heard the sound of the crystal in the wind and I followed it."

"I heard it too," Rian said.

[27]

Curtser stood very still, studying his companions. "I don't know about the sound you followed," he said, "and I do not know anything about crystals but I do have instinct. I know we are exactly where we are supposed to be. I know we are to follow the passage."

Deetra studied Curtser thoughtfully. There was a strength to the young man which she suddenly admired. She felt ashamed that she had not noticed it before, had been so critical of him. To have a crystal was not everything. Hanta had chosen him she was certain, or else he would not be with them.

"Lead the way," Deetra said confidently.

Rian nodded in agreement.

Curtser eyed his companions appreciatively and started for the passageway.

Deetra counted their steps. The first twenty-five were set in total darkness and then she lost count. High up the passage walls rays of white light burst through honeycombed openings in the rock. The tunnel took on an eerie effect—tall and dark with the weight of their shadows and yet light enough to see and follow the sharp angles as the passage twisted and turned through the rock. The silence was deafening, yet alive as each step seemed to echo back at them. Then the passage narrowed. Deetra and Rian followed Curtser, moving sideways, ducking to enter a widened chamber. Curtser held out his arms and stopped.

There were two parallel passages ahead.

"Do you hear anything?" he asked them both.

"No."

"I mean, do you hear the crystal?"

Both Deetra and Rian listened. In the absolute stillness of the passage they agreed that there was a soft hum and told Curtser.

Curtser studied the passages ahead and turned to look

about him; to his companions; to the patterns of light and darkness that filled the area. No one spoke for what seemed a long while.

"What hour of the day do you suppose it is?" Curtser asked.

Deetra recalled that it was nearly sunset when they entered the cave. They had to have travelled for at least an hour, perhaps two since then.

The light!

The light was white, brilliant and clear as Deetra had seen it on occasion when Hanta was near. It was not sunlight. It was the crystal's light. She thought of Ian and called out to him in her thoughts. Why had he let them wander so far. He had said that they were to follow him closely and yet how could they follow him in a sandstorm when they could not see where they were going. Then she remembered how she had followed the sound of the crystal and come upon the cave. The crystal and Ian were One. Sounds of the crystal were all about them now. Her awareness seemed to magnify it. The sound! The crystal! Ian! He was here! Unseen but here!

Never had Deetra exposed her crystal to anyone but now, instinctively she reached in her pouch and drew it out, holding it to the light. It seemed to blend with it, draw at it. The light in the passage grew more intense, so bright that her own flesh seemed to become transparent in it.

"Deetra . . . Deetra where is Curtser?" Rian called out next to her.

It was as though the question in Rian's voice materialized and they could see Curtser in the passageway off to the right, a thin film of a ghostlike shape. Then suddenly, they saw Curtser turn and hurry back toward them.

Deetra returned her crystal to her pouch.

Curtser appeared in the passage opening, an astonished expression on his face.

"What is going on around here?" he asked, studying the surprise on Deetra and Rian's face. "I went into the passageway to explore what was ahead. Then suddenly I felt you both there, but neither of you were. Then I heard you call, but not in voice and yet it felt that I heard you."

"The crystal," Deetra said. "It must have been you saw us and heard us through the crystal."

"We saw you too," Rian said.

"And the light?" Curtser asked.

"The crystal's light," Deetra said, "and that light as well," she added, pointing to the honeycombed opening above their heads.

Curtser looked up anxiously. "It's coming from outside the cave," he said, "not inside. In the passage," he said slowly as if remembering. "I heard something else. A rumbling of sorts. I believe this passage will take us outside—to the light."

Rian drew in a deep breath. The others turned to him.

"You've heard it before," Deetra said for him.

"Yes."

"Where?" Curtser asked.

"It's the Askans," Rian said uneasily.

"How do you know that?"

"The Elder's contemplation used to call them. It's the sounds of creation."

"Did you see them?"

"No."

"Did you hear them?"

"No. Only the rumble—like drums."

Deetra who had been too astonished to speak now asked: "What else do you know of the Askans?"

"Only that they serve the Silent One . . and that they are the masters of the elements, of the universe, and of the crystal's force."

"We could go back," Curtser said quickly.

Deetra studied the boy. "Could we? Where would we go? Back down the mountainside to the village? I think not."

"Deetra's right," Rian said, "we are committed . . each of us in our own way."

Curtser seemed relieved. "Then let us continue our journey," he said. "I am sure we are almost there."

CHAPTER 3

Curtser had assessed the near end of their journey correctly. It seemed that it was only minutes before the three travellers stood with clasped hands in the blinding white light just outside the tunnel.

At first there seemed to be nothing to see but the light. Its brilliance was dazzling; so intense that Deetra felt dizzy, gripping the boys hands as tightly as she could to steady herself. It enveloped them; moved around and through them, pulsing as if alive and knowing. It was taking them over, making them One with It. The light had intelligence! It was an entity, a Being or a Beingness. The rumbling was not drumlike but a heartbeat—their heartbeats or It. Deetra could not be sure. Somewhere deep inside of herself she felt herself scream: "IAN!"

Gradually, as though the light were a mist it rolled back. Before them stood the iridescent figure of Ian. His face bore a pleased expression.

"You have done well," he said. His voice was his voice, yet not a voice at all. "You have arrived at your destination of your own free will, your own choosing. Because you have arrived together, you will learn and grow together. You are bound to each other and yet you are individual as I am bound to you and yet I am myself."

As Deetra listened to Ian she felt gentleness and love.

It was as though a part of her reached out to him with great tenderness but she held back.

Ian saw this but said nothing.

"Where are we?" Curtser asked. And his voice like Ians' was not a voice, yet it was.

"You are on the summit of the crystal," Ian answered. "It is the world between the worlds where the Askan's dwell. Look at yourselves."

For the first time since they entered the light, they looked at one another. They were as Ian, transparent and prismatic; they themselves etheric beings, communicating telepathically.

"I cannot stay with you," Ian said, "so listen carefully. The land that you are to venture into is unlike the village below and yet like it as well. The differences and likenesses you will discover in time. Already you have learned much."

"Will we see Hanta?" Rian asked.

"That's not for me to say," Ian answered.

"Is he here?" Curtser asked.

"He is everywhere. You need only think of him."

"You mean, he is everywhere in thought," Curtser said again.

"I mean, he is everywhere."

Deetra's gaze met Ians'. She understood. It was how they had found the cave. She had thought of Hanta, of Ian; had heard the sound in the wind and followed it. She need only think of him now and he would be there, perhaps not visibly but be there all the same. She remembered how she had felt Ian's presence in the tunnel. Did he have the same power as Hanta? No. She remembered early on their journey how Ian had called Hanta a perfect channel, himself not as close to the source as Hanta. He had also said that she, Curtser and Rian were there to become channels. It was the fate which awaited them.

"Remember," Ian said, first to Deetra directly and

then to the boys, "you are the path. Only a fool looks for a path outside of himself."

"But where are we to go?" Curtser asked.

"Follow your instincts Curtser. Your instincts are keen."

"And what do I follow?" Rian asked.

"You have knowledge stored away which the Elders gave you."

"But I know of nothing."

"The knowledge is there just the same. You remembered the symbol on the cave wall, didn't you?"

Ian had been with them in the cave.

"And you, Deetra," he said ever so softly. "Your path is your sensitivity. The attribute that each of you has will open the way to your inner vision. Each helping the other and thereby learning from each other."

"But there is nothing here but light. Where are we to go?" Curtser asked again.

Ian did not answer. In the long silence Deetra looked about. What was once seemingly all light now revealed form. In the distance there appeared to be a city, a beautiful glowing dome-shaped building rising from the center of it. She pointed to her discovery.

Ian smiled, and for a moment the tenderness of his smile directed at Deetra filled all space; his gaze was on her and in her, both pain and pleasure. She lowered her eyes.

"Now all of you see the city," Ian said. "Deetra saw it first because she is sensitive to the invisible. Therein lies the secret to creation. First there is the vision and the substance follows. So you see we make our own worlds and everything in it. You can change anything or improve it to suit yourself. In the land of the crystal happenings are nearly simultaneous to the vision. The village from where we came is in another dimension. Although creation works the same way there it requires time to materialize. Here time functions differently.

"No day or night," Rian said thoughtfully.

"You remember," Ian added. "When you were a small child Rian, you were told all the secrets of life. They are stored away inside of you, waiting for experience to draw them out."

Curtser had been listening uneasily, trying to assess the distance between them and the city. It appeared to be many miles away.

Ian read his thoughts "The distance does not exist," he said. "But because you do not know its non-existence, it does. You Curtser have the keenest of minds and the greatest courage. It will be your task to realize the truth."

"But how?"

"Practice being Soul."

"But I don't know what soul is."

"It is that part within you that 'knows'. It sees existence exactly as it is. Learn to look for the light and listen to the sound."

"But I don't have a crystal like the others."

"The crystal is merely a tool. Here all life is within the crystal. Your greatest asset here is your courage. You are bold and adventuresome. Lead Rian and Deetra to the city."

As Ian finished speaking his image faded as though being absorbed into the light.

"But what of Moonwalk and Awakening Day?" Curtser shouted, trying to hold Ian in their presence.

Ian was gone.

"We're on Moonwalk," Rian said softly, "Awakening Day awaits in the city ahead."

With Ian gone it was time for the three travellers to move on towards the city far in the distance ahead of them.

[*35*]

Curtser was particularly glad. The environment seemed less dreamlike and more real. The mist had subsided, rolled back to reveal towering mountains to each side of the giant red-rock plateau they were now crossing.

The tall lean youth walked proudly in the lead. Rian and Deetra followed. There was nothing awesome or mystifying about the way ahead. The pathway was obvious, clearly marked and defined not unlike the way into their own village far down the mountain.

There were signs that other travellers had come that way and occasionally Curtser called out a comment to the others. "It hasn't been long since someone else has walked this path," or "see the sandle marks there." And he would pause and point to a definite indentation in the shallow sand. Indeed he became so at ease and comfortable that he had begun to hum a tune which they had often heard sung while working the wheat fields:

Oh, a working day is play, is play

when all the farmers blend their hay

and toil not too harsh a day

then oh, a working day is play, is play.

Rian, with Deetra remained silent behind him. Except for Curtser's song there was silence about them. The landscape had a peculiar hush to it—no woodland creatures or birds. The sky appeared to be dull, empty space, colorless except for the mist which loomed like a heavy dark cloak against the mountain tops, and the etheric misty city set far into the horizon. The way was different, they knew, than any they had travelled before and the difference seemed to caution them.

Quite suddenly Curtser stopped and turned to his companions.

"How do you know this is moonwalk?" he asked Rian.

Rian who had been moving along deep in thought studied Curtser with a long look. "The Elders spoke of the cave and where it led," he said thoughtfully.

"Were they speaking to you directly when they said it?"

"No." Rian was quiet as if remembering before he went on. "It is part of the sacred scripture they read aloud."

"Do you remember how it went?"

"The crystal bearers will find its light. Dark will turn into light. At the end of the passage between the worlds, the journeymen will meet with an envoy who will point the way to the illuminated city." Rian paused, carefully choosing from memory the proper words to continue. "Along the way they will be visited by the inhabitants of the inbetween worlds. Herein will be the tests and the testing grounds one must pass through in order to enter the city."

Deetra was listening with great interest. She waited, as if expecting the younger boy to continue.

"Why didn't you tell us this before?" Curtser asked.

"I only now remembered."

"What else?" Deetra asked. "There must be more."

"Nothing else comes to mind."

"Who are these inhabitants of the inbetween worlds?" Curtser asked. "We have seen no one."

Rian shrugged his shoulders. "Perhaps they're invisible."

"We are not invisible," Curtser said, "so there is no reason for them to be."

"Perhaps reason is not valid here," Deetra said. "If we are inbetween the worlds, reason may not exist."

"She's right," Rian said.

Curtser appeared annoyed. "I am not a mystic nor a

crystal bearer and yet I saw the crystal's light along with you. Either the scripture is wrong or you have remembered it incorrectly."

"Or it could be Curtser," Deetra said quite slowly, "that because you travel with crystal bearers you share in witnessing the crystal's light."

Curtser lowered his eyes. Instinctively he knew what she said to be true and the knowledge of it humbled him.

"But you are with us to share and help us by your courage and natural instincts," Deetra said earnestly, wanting to lift the boys spirits.

"We'd better be on our way," Rian said.

Just then some movement came from somewhere forward on the path. Whatever it was it seemed to have breath to it and it seemed to be running toward them.

Curtser stood in front of his companions and bravely held out his arms in protective gesture.

Listening . . . watching . . . Deetra's heart stood still. One moment there was only movement and the next there stood an old woman, a dark shawl draped about her head and shoulders, blending with a greyish blouse and skirt which covered her to the ground. She seemed to expect them and ran over to them.

"We must hurry! We must hurry!" she said in a hoarse voice. "The savior comes!"

"Who are you?" Curtser asked. His voice was steady but he appeared somewhat shaken by the sudden appearance of the old woman.

"No time . . . No time!" the woman said, waving her hands in a dispairing manner. "If you are not saved you will be killed. You will burn in hell!"

Deetra reached for Curtser's arm and squeezed it. The boy turned his attention momentarily to Deetra and when he looked back the old woman was gone.

"Where did she go?"

"She's one of the inhabitants of the inbetween worlds," Deetra said.

"How do you know that?" Curtser snapped.

"Where did she come from and where has she gone," Deetra answered.

"The inhabitants of the inbetween worlds only exist as aberrations. The aberrations disappear when the attention is removed from them." Rian said the words slowly and carefully.

"I don't believe it," Curtser said.

"It's in the scriptures," Rian said.

"It can't be," Curtser said again.

"But it is," Deetra said firmly.

"And I suppose you saw the scripture too."

"No. But I know it," Deetra said firmly.

Curtser studied the girl. Although he had a deep respect for her, he could not accept what he did not know himself. "I must have some proof," he said. "I'm going to look for the old woman. You can come with me, or remain here as you wish."

Deetra turned to Rian. "We were told to stay together," the boy said. "Ian told us that since we arrived together, we would learn together."

Deetra did not want to follow Curtser now. Inwardly she knew and understood the truth in the scriptures. She wanted to continue on to the city which still seemed far in the distance. She remembered Ian's words, telling them that there was no time nor space; that the distance between them and the city did not exist. Why then were they not there? Why did the city appear to be so distant?

Curtser reached for her hand, clasping it tightly. "It is my understanding that we are here to experience the inbetween worlds," he said persuasively. It seems to me if we avoid meeting them we are missing the experience and who knows what other fortification we would miss. Is not the experience all preparation for Awakening Day? If experience were not necessary wouldn't we have left the cave and immediately entered the city with no knowledge of the inbetween worlds?"

Deetra withdrew her hand from the boy. What he had said made sense although something still deep within cautioned her. She called on Ian in her mind for guidance. With all her strength she imagined his face and in her imagining she waited for a sign. He seemed to nod lovingly.

"All right, Curtser," she said. "I will follow you for now. But if you decide at any time not to continue on to the city, I will leave and go on without you."

"Agreed," Curtser said confidentally.

"Agreed," Rian said.

★ ★ ★

Curtser moved with quick, sure steps up the winding path occasionally calling out for the old woman. Although they saw no one it was as though the little band was following some unseen leader. It was hurrying them. Suddenly Curtser broke into a run. His swift movement carried him almost immediately out of sight, disappearing around a bend in the road. Deetra and Rian kept their pace, walking quickly until they came to the bend where Curtser had disappeared.

They stopped.

There were voices. Not Curtser's voice but a strong, deep but gentle voice speaking. They could not hear what the man was saying.

A thrill rose in Deetra, a peculiar tinkling which began in her feet and travelled through her body. She turned to Rian who was suddenly trembling next to her. She reached for his hand.

"I'm frightened," the boy whispered.

"I am as well," said Deetra, "but Curtser is out there. We must go see."

[*40*]

They rounded the bend.

Standing on a high rock towering above a circle of people was a tall, slim, brown-skinned man dressed in flowing pink robes. His head was covered with a pink turban. The faces of those about him were humbled and reverant. The old woman was next to Curtser directly in front. Deetra could not see her friend's face.

"Your sins shall be forgiven you and the kingdom of heaven is yours'," the voice said, rising from the stone platform. "I am the way and the truth, the Pink Prince of Love. All who come to me will know the full joy and meaning of love for I offer you ALL."

Just then the Pink Prince raised his arms. All within the circle about him fell to their knees, except Curtser who remained standing, looking on curiously. The Pink Prince seemed not to notice him, his head tilted up to an empty sky.

"Oh King of Kings surrender these souls and give them unto me their savior in love," the man dressed in pink said.

A huge clap of thunder sounded above the crowd.

Suddenly Curtser turned about, saw Deetra and Rian and hurried over to them where the three watched as the Prince continued.

"As ruler of this universe the strength of these people is mine. I will nourish them with the adoration they pour upon me and all life will be sustained."

Thunder, accompanied with a jagged streak of lightening bolted over the Pink one's head.

"I control all," he shouted.

A terrible moan rang through the circle of kneeling people. Suddenly their images shivered and shook, vibrating. Deetra looked up to the Pink Prince at the same time as they did. But now he was gone.

Gradually, as though caught in a dream, the grey-

[*41*]

looking gathering arose. The circle scattered as many wandered off in various directions. The old woman turned to Curtser and approached.

"You must come with me," she said to Curtser.

Deetra noted the deep set lines of the old woman's face. They reminded her of ripples on a pond when the wind blew. Her eyes were piercing dark pools set in red sockets.

"Who are you?" Deetra asked.

"I am Olivia," she answered still gazing at Curtser. "You must come with me."

"What do you want with me?" Curtser asked sharply.

"He cannot go with you," Deetra answered for him. "He is on a mission to meet with Hanta, the Silent One."

The old woman wavered but did not move her eyes from Curtser. "You were in the circle of the Pink Prince. You belong to him now. You must come quickly. He awaits you."

"I belong to no one," Curtser said, taking a step backwards. "I am on my way to the City of Light to attend Awakening Day."

The old woman laughed. "There is no such place. The Prince of Love is all there is. Nothing else exists. If you do not come with me now, you will perish, all of you."

"Enough," Deetra snapped angrily. "You are a creature of the inbetween worlds. You do not exist. You are merely energy, the energy of illusion."

"Am I now," the old woman cackled. Suddenly she grabbed for Curtser and held his arm tightly with an iron grip.

"I can not move," Curtser yelled.

In a flash, Deetra remembered the crystal. She reached in her pouch and drew it out, extending it at arm's length in front of the old woman's face. "Be gone," she shouted.

The image of the old woman began to shimmer while still holding tightly to Curtser's arm.

"She's taking me," Curtser called out. Then his image began to shimmer too. A moment later they were both gone.

Deetra flung at the empty space in front of her but it was too late. Curtser was gone, disappeared with the old woman. The crystal had worked but it had worked against her friend Curtser as well.

Suddenly she remembered Rian. He had not stepped forward nor said anything. Quickly turning about she saw that he was gone. She called out to him: "Rian . . . Rian where are you?"

There was no answer.

Rian had disappeared as well.

She was alone.

★　★　★

Deetra sat leaning against a rock staring blankly into space where the Pink Prince and his followers had been gathered, wondering at what to do. The silence seemed absolute. No one nor no thing stirred and in the stillness there was nothing to do but recall each detail of what had happened time and time again. If only she had remembered to help Curtser withdraw his attention from the old woman she would have been powerless against him. Instead she had used the crystal. The power of it had banished Curtser as well. And Rian? What had happened to Rian? Had the crystal removed him? It seemed unlikely, but she didn't know. Perhaps he had wandered off, or frightened had hidden himself from Olivia's presence. No. That didn't seem likely either. Wondering, she turned the crystal about in her hand and absently held it up to the light. What power did the crystal have?

Then she saw.

Within the refractions of light there were tiny images. When she looked directly into the crystal the images disappeared. But with her vision defused she saw something in its light. Gradually she understood. Whatever she thought took shape there. She recalled sitting beneath the oak tree in the field near her father's house, examining the crystal and seeing the image of herself, Ian and Hanta as one. And the same humming sound she had heard then seemed to come from within her now and flow without. The image of Hanta appeared. He stood above her now as he had then, only now he turned to where the Pink Prince had been and motioned her to follow him. Deetra rose and went to the rock platform. The Silent One bent down and pointed to a symbol etched into the rock—a pentagon and a dagger. On the dagger's handle was another symbol, a cross with a dazzling pink jewel set in the center of it.

What did it mean?

Studying the symbols on the rock Deetra suddenly felt dizzy and separate, a feeling of flowing out of herself. She looked to Hanta and the illusion was gone. Then she saw the Silent One do a peculiar thing. He stepped into the rock as though it were liquid and not solid. He sank deeper and deeper into it. Amazed, Deetra's mind went completely still. Hanta stepped out of the rock and onto the ground next to her. He took her hand. Immediately they both sank waist high into the earth and began to walk through it as one would walk though water. As they walked, they came to a tree. Hanta moved right through it and next Deetra. Yes. Now she knew. She had known all along that the inhabitants of the inbetween worlds were illusion but the world they lived in was illusion as well.

Hanta smiled at her understanding; let go of her hand and kissed her lightly on the cheek. At the touch of his lips a flash of light went through her. It was the crystal's light and as he disappeared into its brilliance, he also showed her what to do. The light was Hanta but also the vision of the crystal. It was the tool to see through illusion. And now she remembered that Ian had told them that very thing when they had first begun their journey.

The tiny images she had seen before Hanta's appearance now became clear to her. She held up the crystal again and thought deeply into herself, wondering at Curtser's whereabouts. Then she saw him.

Curtser was standing in the middle of an empty room with no windows or doors. The walls appeared to be made of stone but in the light of the crystal Deetra saw that the walls were not walls at all but rather a transparent, film-like image of grey stone walls. It was an illusion set up for his perception. He could walk right through it if he knew, but Deetra could see that Curtser did not know it. She tried calling to him through the crystal. For an instant she saw that he looked about as though he heard her. She called again, trying to move an image of herself through the walls to show him as Hanta had shown her but he could not see her. She reached for him; tried to take his hand and although a look of hope crossed his face, she saw that he did not believe her presence. A look of dispair and resignation returned to his expression.

How could she help him?

Then she thought of Rian. She turned her thoughts strongly to him. At first there was nothing. Then about her she heard the crystal hum and she turned her inner voice to it, riding upon it. "Rian . . Rian remember the crystal. Use it now," she called. Instantly she saw an image of Rian, a tiny image at first, then larger. She called to him again, "use the crystal," she said, and then she saw Rian reach into his pouch and withdraw his crystal, holding it up to light.

"Deetra," he said, returning her call. "I'm in a strange land where there is nothing."

"What do you see?" Deetra asked the boy.

"I see nothing, Curtser is not here. No one is here.

There is nothing here, not a tree, nor a bush, nor a rock and no one."

"I found Curtser," she told him. "He's locked in a room with stone walls, but the walls are illusion. He's not locked in at all. He only believes himself to be."

"Did you talk to him?"

"He won't believe that I am there," she said. "But what about you? How did you get where you are?"

"I can't remember," Rian said.

"But you must."

"I know." The boy paused thoughtfully, as if trying to remember. "It has to do with the Pink Prince. I was trying to remember him, about him, when I disappeared."

"The Pink Prince is a master of illusion," she said. "Hanta was with me. He showed me the illusion of this world. We walked through rock, into the earth and together we passed right through a tree."

"But there is something else," Rian said. "Something I need to remember in order to free myself."

"But what's holding you. I see nothing."

"A feeling . . . a feeling of some kind."

"What kind of a feeling?" she asked.

Rian was very still. For a moment his image faded and then grew stronger again. "In the scriptures," he said, "it says that traps are formed by the feeling elements in man."

"But it is all right to feel," Deetra said.

"But when we become attached to our feelings for someone or something, we become trapped by them."

"Then let go of your attachment," she said, suddenly annoyed at the boy.

"I don't know how."

"Well, just let go."

"How?"

Deetra grew quiet and thoughtful. She walked over to a tree. Seeing it as solid, she touched it, patted it and withdrew her hand. Then she saw the tree as soft and pliable and when she touched the tree again, she squeezed it between her fingers. She put her hand right through the tree and studied her fingers protruding through the other side. If Rian could have a change of feelings then he could be free of his attachment.

Returning her attention to the crystal once more, she called to Rian again.

"What have you learned Deetra?" he asked.

"What is your feeling about?" she asked.

"Love," Rian said. "The Pink Prince is the symbol of love to the between world inhabitants. He is their saviour."

Before Deetra could answer him, an image of the Pink Prince appeared before Rian and wrapped him in his robes. Rian seemed to be swallowed up by him and was no longer visible.

"Rian!" Deetra called.

There was no answer. Only an image of the robes belonging to the Pink Prince was visible and that image was fading. Rian was trapped by his feeling for him.

The light diminished. A sudden panic gripped Deetra and the crystal became lifeless in her hand. Both Rian and Curtser were trapped and she didn't know how to help them.

Disturbed, Deetra sat down to think. She thought of Hanta and of Ian but they did not come to her now. She turned her thoughts back to her village and to her father, the bond of love between them. She remembered working in the fields with him, listening to the song that the worker's sung. Curtser had sung that song too before the old woman had appeared. She hummed it and then put the words to it.

> Oh, a working day is play, is play
> when all the farmers blend their hay

and toil not too harsh a day
then oh, a working day is play, is play.
The song seemed to lighten her spirits and she sang it
again and again. Then she had an idea. She pulled the
crystal from her pouch and called up an image of Curtser.
He was sitting on the dirt floor in the room with stone
walls, his chin resting on his knees. She began to sing the
working song to him. Over and over again she sang:
Oh, a working day is play, is play
when all the farmers blend their hay
and toil not too harsh a day
then oh, a working day is play, is play.
Suddenly the lad sat upright and looked about. He
began to sing the tune, softly at first, then boldly. He arose
to his feet singing loudly off key. She watched as he strut
about the room singing. Then Curtser did a strange and
courageous thing. He drew back his arm, his hand
clenched into a fist and attacked the wall with all his
strength. Instead of colliding with something solid, Curtser had pushed himself through the wall. He was free.

"Curtser!" Deetra yelled, jumping joyfully to her
feet. The boy was standing just a few feet away, a look of
amazement on his face.

"Curtser, you did it!" she called again.

"I started singing and . . . ."

"I know, I watched you," Deetra said.

"You watched me," the boy repeated astonished.

"Yes, in the crystal. I sang to you. You heard the song
and joined in. Your attention was removed from the illusion and you broke yourself free."

"Is that what happened . . . really," the boy asked,
still somewhat dazed.

"Really!"

Curtser told Deetra how he had been transported

seemingly into another dimension by the old woman Olivia; how she had sealed him into the stone room by means of magic, and how Olivia had told him that the Pink Prince required his energy to do his work in the village. That was why he was held captive.

Deetra who had been listening attentively now bolted to her feet. "What of Rian?" she asked.

"Isn't he here?"

"No. He disappeared the same time you did." Then she told Curtser how she had talked with Rian through the crystal; how he was being held by his feelings for the Pink Prince and how he had disappeared into the Prince's robes while she was talking with him.

"We must find him," Curtser said bravely.

"We will. But first, what else do you know about the Pink Prince?"

"Nothing. Olivia didn't say anymore than he needed my energy to work in the village."

"Awakening Day," Deetra said thoughtfully. "It has to do with Awakening Day, and the village people's preparations for it." Deetra explained how the Pink Prince was the master of illusion and how Hanta had showed her the depth of his power.

"But how could his power be used in the village? His domain is here; his power is here."

"Do you remember what Ian told us when we entered this land from the cave?"

"That there was no time nor space," Curtser said, remembering.

"Yes, but he also told us that this world was like the village, only different, and that we would discover the differences and the likenesses."

"Meaning that the village is subject to the illusion of this world only differently," Curtser said.

"Yes, at least seemingly different. The village is another plane of existence. The illusion of this plane is obvious. In the village illusion is more difficult to grasp."

If only Rian was here he could tell us what the scriptures say about it," Curtser said.

"That's it!" Deetra held up the crystal to the light and called out to Rian.

There was no image and no answer.

"Try again," Curtser said.

Holding the crystal, Deetra summoned all her imaginative powers to focus on Rian. She thought of him coming upon her when she had communicated with Hanta along the trail up on the mountain early in their journey; how together they had followed the hum of silence to find the cave, and all the while she filled herself with love for the younger boy. "Rian . . . Rian!" she called softly but intensely. "We need your help. Use the crystal."

Gradually the crystal in Deetra's hand took on new life, colors darted from it and danced in spiral motion. Then Rian appeared. "I can't get away," he said.

"We are trying to find a way to help you," Curtser said bravely.

"You made it back," Rian said.

"Yes, and so will you. But first we need some information. What is the difference between this world and the village?" Curtser asked Rian.

"All power filters down from above," Rian said. "The power here comes from above." Then he stopped and turned away. The Pink Prince was suddenly beckoning to him.

"Don't go Rian," Deetra called to the boy. But it was as though he was hypnotized and in a trance. "Rian! Rian!" she called again, but he did not hear. He disappeared.

"Well, we got our answer," Curtser said.

Deetra was still looking into the crystal's light for Rian and did not respond.

"If all power filters downward, then the power also exists in the village," Curtser said as if thinking aloud. "That provides the sameness that Ian spoke of and . . . ."

Deetra held up her hand.

"But the power dissipates and becomes more coarse as it descends," Deetra added, putting the crystal away and turning her full attention to Curtser. "So the powers of the Pink Prince can be used in the village."

"The information doesn't tell us how or what to do to stop him" Curtser said.

"But it does," Deetra said earnestly.

"How?"

"How do you think the Pink Prince will get to the village?" Deetra asked as though thinking aloud.

"The same way we did?"

"No. Not through the cave. He will use his powers. Remember time and space here functions differently. He will simply project himself."

"In what way?"

"In the same way I projected the working song to you, or as we just communicated with Rian," Deetra said.

"You mean the Prince has a crystal?"

"He doesn't need one. The crystal is merely a tool. The Pink Prince is the Lord of Illusion. He simply projects himself downward."

"What do we do?" Curtser asked. "Do we summon the Prince in the crystal as we did Rian?"

"That would be too dangerous," Deetra said. "To summon the Prince might give him power over us. We must think this out and plan carefully," she said thoughtfully.

"The old woman said that he needed my energy," the boy said.

"That would be to use you as a link with those you have a bond."

"Like my father the miller."

"Yes, but the Prince doesn't have you anymore. He can't use you."

"Then he will use Rian."

A cold chill ran through Deetra. Rian had developed some mysterious feeling for the Prince. He would be used definitely, but with whom. The boy was an orphan.

"The Elders," Curtser said, anticipating her thoughts. "Rian's only true bond in the village is with the Elders—Sarpent in particular."

Deetra had the same feeling that she had had when the old woman first appeared to them, a tinkling sensation which travelled down her spine to her toes. She knew what Curtser said was true. She remembered Ian's explanation that her illusions manifested swiftly, simultaneously to the vision, but that in the village which was another dimension, more time was required for materialization. She wished only that there would be enough time.

"We need a link, someone to communicate with in the village," Deetra said absently.

"My father," Curtser suggested.

"Does he have a crystal?"

"No. Then Sarpent—surely he has one."

Deetra thought of Sarpent's forbidding face and of the Pink Prince who would try to control him. She would rather have another link, someone with whom she would be comfortable.

"My father," she said at last. "He has a crystal. Just before I left the village he showed it to me. He told me of the village pledge."

"What pledge?"

She told Curtser of the pledge that the people of the village had made long ago—to serve the Great One as a channel for the Divine Force. It was the reason for Awakening day—to bring those souls forward who were ready.

Curtser listened intensely, thoughtfully. The story was familiar to him only he couldn't remember where he had heard it, perhaps long ago when he was a child.

"What do you think?" Deetra asked, studying the far-off expression on the boy's face.

"I feel as though I am dreaming. Life is suddenly become so incredible," Curtser said absently.

"I know, but dream or not Rian is trapped and the Pink Prince is about to create havoc in the village. We must plan our strategy."

Curtser walked over to the boulder which the Prince had stood upon and studied the dagger etched into the rock. The tiny pink jewel set into the handle glared back at him. Suddenly, he reached down and plucked it out.

"Well, look at this!" he said.

Deetra watched in amazement. Hanta had pointed it out to her but she had not tried to remove it. She had assumed it had been deeply embedded into the rock.

Curtser held the jewel up to the light. "Do you suppose it's a pink crystal?" he asked.

Deetra joined Curtser in looking into its light. Instead of containing the colors of the prism it had a reddish hue. Objects seen through its reflections appeared transparent. As the light refractions touched something it became invisible. Suddenly Curtser was invisible.

"Curtser!" Deetra yelled.

"I'm here, and I see what's happening." Then he turned the pink stone's red light so that it shone on Deetra. "And now you are invisible," he said. "Whatever the light touches becomes invisible."

"Illusion!" Deetra said. "I imagine that's how the Pink Prince appears and disappears."

"Then why doesn't he have it with him? If the jewel

[*53*]

was his power wouldn't he carry it about?" Curtser asked.

"I don't know." Deetra was suddenly frightened and looked about as though expecting the Prince to appear.

"Look here!" Curtser yelled. Turning the pink stone about between his fingers Curtser demonstrated a peculiar scene. Turning it one way the light seemed to collect matter and turning it the other it seemed to repel it. Holding it still everything the light touched became invisible. It had three functions.

"Deetra try looking at it through your crystal," Curtser said anxiously, continuing to slowly turn the pink stone clockwise between his fingers.

Deetra held up the crystal. A cold chill ran through her. Within the blend of light she saw the Pink Prince standing between them. His face was iridescent and demanding.

"Are you prepared to die?" the Prince asked her.

Deetra was spellbound. It was as though eternity filled the moment and she could not move nor speak.

"No one has lived to share my secrets," the Prince said in loud voice. "And so you shall know them." His words trailed off into a loud roar, and his countenance changed from pink to a deep blood red, darkening almost to total blackness. Pictures of the village people appeared and disappeared—her father, her neighbors, Sarpent and the Elders. Each held a lifeless pebble in outstretched hand. They were the crystal-bearers of the village only the crystals were turned to stone. Wrapped about each was a loose flowing pink robe and everything they touched became dull and lifeless. And then Deetra saw a picture of herself. She was struggling inside a dark cave. The image sharply caught her attention and she remembered the cave she had found while searching for Ian. "Ian! Ian!" she called deeply within herself. The image of herself and the cave began to shimmer, fading. Then she saw Curtser and felt his comforting arm about her.

"Are you all right?" he asked·

Deetra nodded.

"I don't know what you saw but from the terrible expression on your face I thought you to be in danger so I put the pink stone away."

"Where? Where did you put it?" she asked, still visibly shaken.

"In my pocket."

"You mustn't keep it. I saw the Prince. He showed me what he intends to accomplish in the village." She related to Curtser the images she had seen.

"But we can't leave it here," Curtser said, "It is a symbol of his power. It may prove useful to us."

Deetra shuddered at the thought, remembering how she had felt spellbound in the Prince's presence. She didn't dare to think of what might have happened if Curtser had not put the pink stone away.

"We will be careful with it," Curtser said earnestly. "But something tells me we must keep it."

Deetra thought of Ian; how she had called to him in her vision and she remembered that Ian had told them that Curtser had keen instinct and that his instinct would serve them on their journey. Although still uncertain if they should keep the stone, she agreed.

★ ★ ★

Deetra tried to relax, to sit and think, to shed the feelings of fear from her thoughts but the more she struggled within herself, the more she could not forget the presence of the Pink Prince, his threat that she would die and the knowledge that Curtser in keeping the Prince's stone had pocketed the very power she now feared. She thought of Rian and how he had become attached to his feeling for the

Prince and was trapped by that feeling. Was she to suffer a similar fate; was Curtser next? What of the village people? If she was doomed, were they also doomed? No! She could not let it be so. She was here in this land of illusion to learn and to prepare herself for the great Awakening Day. If she failed there were many who could be affected by her failure. "Oh please, dear Hanta give me strength within myself," she pleaded softly aloud. "Please help me!"

It was as if the words drew some power towards her. In that instant she thought of her father and remembered that she had decided with Curtser that they would contact him through the crystal. She sat erect and looked to Curtser who was sitting a short distance away, watching her.

"We will use the crystal now," she said, motioning him nearer. Then she drew it from her pouch, held it up to the light and with all her strength called to her father.

She saw him almost immediately. He was walking through the village on the same road she had travelled to Tower Rock the morning she had begun her journey. His steps were hurried, his expression serious and he looked straight ahead with full attention to where ever he was going.

The crystal hummed loudly as though part of a raging wind. She called to her father. He stopped, looked about and listened. "Father . . . father, the crystal father." She watched him turn about, step off the roadway into a grove of trees. He withdrew his crystal and then listened again.

"Father! Father! It is Deetra," she said within the humming crystal.

"Deetra!"

"Yes. There is trouble!"

"I know. I know," he said. "Where are you?"

"On Moonwalk—on our way to the golden city." Then she told him of the land of illusion, of the inhabitants there, of the Pink Prince and Rian's entrapment.

[56]

"The Pink Prince is already here," he said. He has turned many of the villagers against the Elders. Sarpent is in battle with him now and I go to assist him."

"What will you do?"

"I do not know," he said, pausing. "Perhaps you can help my daughter."

"I know his plan," Deetra said, not allowing herself to acknowledge a low feeling which seemed ready to pounce on her.

"Which is?" her father asked.

"To take away the power of the crystal from the crystal bearers."

"And how will he accomplish that?"

"The Pink Prince is the master of illusion," she said, uncertain of how to explain.

Her father remained quiet and thoughtful, looking deeply into the crystal at his daughter. "Are you afraid Deetra?" he asked.

"A little," she answered, nodding, hesitantly.

"Well you must not allow yourself to fear him. Remember it was you who told me that Rian was trapped by his attachment to a feeling for the Prince. It is the only way he can have power over you . . . over any of us. It is the only way the Prince can remove the power from the crystal."

Deetra was comforted by her father's encouragement. She told him of the pink jewel Curtser had taken from the dagger in the rock.

"I don't know of it but I agree that he was right to keep it. It may help us somehow. Let me think on it. But now I must hurry. Sarpent is in danger," he said. "When so many people are fearful, they weaken Sarpent's power and strengthen the Prince's. So be cautious, but do not fear lest you become an instrument for fear itself. Do you understand my daughter?"

"Yes."

"Then remain knowing that illusion is merely illusion. Your strength is needed now. I will call on you when I join with Sarpent."

The light in the crystal faded.

Deetra's father was gone.

CHAPTER 4

Sarpent stood on the stone platform at Bell Rock with arms folded across his chest, his back to the other Elders who formed a semi-circle directly behind him. Directly facing him but a few feet away was the Pink Prince and next to him was Rian. The silence was bursting with anticipation, eyes locked in willful challenge. Only Rian stirred slightly, unable to look directly at Sarpent or the Elders and instead cast his glance towards the ground where a large circle with a line drawn out of the center of it was deeply etched into the rock. He remembered and yet he did not remember, as if something were holding him back from what he knew.

Deetra and Curtser watched through the crystal.

Thunder and lightning cracked over the Prince's head. Rian trembled and clung to the Prince's feet. The Elders did not budge, seemingly unmoved by the dramatics. It was then that Deetra noticed that the firm set of their jaws and their hard stares were not directed at the Prince but through him. The Prince held up his hands and again the thunder clapped. No one moved, nor flinched except Rian who was now whimpering at the Prince's feet. It was as though the Elders had established an invisible wall and the Prince was endeavoring to break through it.

"Poor Rian," Curtser said compassionately. "Isn't there something we can do to reach him?"

"Perhaps," Deetra said thoughtfully. "If we could transport his attention to the cave where we saw the symbol."

"You mean it would work for him as it did for me when you projected the song into my stone prison."

"Yes."

"Let's try," Curtser said.

Deetra and Curtser used their imaginations to reach back in memory to when the three of them had discovered the cave and the symbol on the wall which Rian had remembered from the platform floor. They directed his hand to the symbol now, encouraging his fingers to trace it as he had done as a child while reminding him of the cave. In dazed fashion Rian responded, touching the symbol lightly, then boldly; his movements more sure. They were reaching him!

Then suddenly, at the moment Rian would have come to his senses, the Prince took the boy's hand, raised him to his feet and wrapped his cloak about him. An instant later they both disappeared.

The Elders relaxed. The invisible wall seemed to melt away. It was then that Deetra saw her father step upon the platform, and addressing Sarpent he told the Elders of his communication with his daughter and of the pink jewel Curtser had removed from the Prince's dagger.

There was a long silence. Sarpent unfolded his arms and looked out toward the village. "The Pink Prince has not gone," he said, "only removed himself to more vulnerable company."

"Have all the crystal bearers been told of his appearance?" Deetra's father, Starn, asked.

"Yes Starn, but some are stronger than others. There are those who will succumb," Sarpent said.

[*60*]

"Does it weaken us?" Starn asked.

"No, it does not weaken us, and yet it does," Sarpent said. "It does not weaken us because each of us must choose for ourselves, but it weakens us in numbers, and the strength that numbers bring."

"What of your daughter Deetra, and Curtser?"

"They are strong," Starn said confidentally. "I will show you." Starn drew out his crystal and held it up to the light. "Are you there my daughter?" he asked.

"And Curtser is with me," she answered immediately. "We witnessed what happened with the Prince. Just prior to his disappearance we tried to reach Rian." She told him of the symbol and how when Rian began to respond the Prince stole him away.

"Do you know what feeling the boy has for the Prince?" Sarpent asked Deetra.

"Not for sure. He fears him, but it seems he also loves him." Deetra was pleased that she could speak so forthright to Sarpent, remembering how she had always avoided him.

"The boy seems to need a feeling of belonging," Sarpent said softly as if to himself. "I have watched that feeling grow in him. It is the trial of an orphan."

"We will reach him somehow," Deetra said confidentally.

Sarpent's face took on a dark and forbidding expression. "Perhaps," he said, "we will see." Then Sarpent drew his crystal from beneath his robe and motioned to the other Elders to do the same. All held their crystals up to the light. A blind array of pale blue light reached between the dimensions, reaching and pulling; the hum of the crystals so intense and the light so blinding.

Then it stopped.

The crystals were put away.

Deetra and Curtser were standing on the platform

facing Sarpent and the Elders and Starn.

Sarpent had transported them to Bell Rock.

"For now we need you here," Sarpent said to Deetra and Curtser.

Deetra looked to her father. His eyes were moist, soft and loving, but he did not speak. She looked to Sarpent who was studying Curtser. His keen eyes flashing about the boy.

"Show me the pink jewel you have taken from the dagger," Sarpent said.

Curtser reached into his pocket and withdrew the jewel and held it out to Sarpent.

"It is not for me to hold the jewel," Sarpent said. "You withdrew it from the dagger. You alone may wield its power."

Deetra was astonished, remembering how she had felt dizzy and separate when she had first seen the jewel with Hanta; how her attention had been drawn from it and how Curtser's attention had been drawn to it. He had discovered its force and shown her its power.

"Show me," Sarpent commanded Curtser. "Show me what you have learned of the jewel."

Curtser held the jewel up to the light. It turned from pink to blood red then nearly black. Everything its light touched became invisible. Then he turned it forward between his fingers—matter, bits of dust, collected itself about the light. He turned it to the other way and the dust scattered away, repelled. Stilling it the invisible happened again.

"The three forces of creation," Sarpent said. "The positive, the negative and the neutralizing forces."

A slow chill ran through Deetra. She had grown to recognize it as a warning, a sensation of fear, but also of something else; something which puzzled and confused her. She lowered her eyes.

[*62*]

"I can see you do not understand," Sarpent said, gently tilting the girl's chin up with his hand. All along you have feared the Pink Prince and in your thoughts you have called his power bad."

He knew what she was thinking.

"Now," Sarpent continued, gently gazing at the girl, "you are confused because the pink jewel which belongs to the Prince possesses the three forces of creation. Listen closely to what I am about to tell you. The powers of the Prince are not evil. They are the forces of matter; the magnet of manifestation." Sarpent paused to study her momentarily. "All things come from the Divine Force," he continued. "The Pink Prince is the Lord of Illusion, but that does not make him evil or to be feared. It is his task to weave spells around people. Were it not for him we could not learn through the experiences of illusion."

Deetra's mind reeled with question. Olivia? The inhabitants of the inbetween worlds and Rian? What of Rian?

Sarpent seemed to read her thoughts. "Hopefully Rian will see through the illusion the Prince has weaved around him. He has the crystal and those who love him to help him break the spell. Although we may be able to help, Rian must help himself. No one can break the illusion of another person."

Deetra remembered how Curtser had broken through his stone prison. What of Olivia who had placed him there?

"As you have already learned, we trap ourselves through our feelings," Sarpent said.

"Yes, but what of Olivia?" Deetra asked.

"Those of the inbetween worlds are entities who used to live here in the physical worlds and died believing illusion was reality. Water seeks its own level. It is only natural that believing illusion they live illusion."

[*63*]

"If Rian were to die while being held by the Pink Prince would he go there?" Curtser asked.

"Yes."

"Does one ever escape the inbetween worlds?" Deetra asked.

"After a time one is born again into this world to try again." Sarpent turned away as if to end the discussion, talking to the Elders in a tone which Deetra could not hear.

"But what of Awakening Day?" Deetra dared to call after him. "What of the Pink Prince and his intentions in the village?"

Sarpent turned toward her momentarily. It was as though the great stern face transformed and became Hanta. A feeling of love poured from him to her and in that instant it was as though she was somewhere strattled between the dimensions of time and space, between the worlds of the crystal; both on her way to the city of light and to the village as well. Then the face became Sarpent again and he turned away, leading the Elders from the platform.

Starn took his daughter's hand and squeezed it lovingly. "We must go to the village," he said. "The law of silence was yet unbroken when I left, but now the Pink Prince is among the people."

"But aren't we breaking the law by speaking?" Curtser asked.

"We are not speaking audibly," Starn answered "It only seems that way. Crystal bearers can easily communicate telepathically."

"But I am not a crystal bearer," Curtser said.

"You hold the jewel of creation," Starn said, "it seems to me that it works quite nicely."

"You mean . . . " Curtser began to question and then stopped himself.

[*64*]

"You didn't need the jewel in the inbetween worlds," Starn suggest. "Perhaps you discovered it to use as a tool here. The power it contains is for you to discover. But this much I know for certain. Although it functions well as an instrument to communicate with crystal bearers it also functions quite differently."

Deetra who had been listening now remembered how the Prince had appeared when she held the crystal's light next to the jewels'. Her eyes met Curtsers'. He had the same thought.

"We must go now," Starn said.

Starn led his daughter and Curtser off the platform, through the empty gathering place below and down the road towards the village. No one spoke and Deetra was glad. She needed time to be alone within herself; time to digest what was happening. She sympathized with Curtser. She too felt she was living an extraordinary dream and the effects of it were changing her. She no longer felt the same about anything she had felt before meeting the crystal and Ian. It seemed so long ago. Where was Ian now? Was he with Hanta on Moonwalk or was he here in the village? As she questioned, the questions seemed strange, as though the village and Moonwalk were really the same place only another dimension of the same.

Then they stopped.

Starn motioned Deetra and Curtser to wait while he went ahead along the road. He disappeared briefly and when he returned there was someone with him.

It was Ian.

The young man smiled in greeting. Curtser jumped forward with extended arm and the two clasped hands. Deetra held back as though expecting him to be a mirage. Then he approached her and took her hands between his. The warmth of his flesh brought tears to Deetra's eyes.

"There is a house ahead where we can rest," Ian said,

letting go of Deetra's hands and turning to the others. "We had best hurry if we're going to reach it before nightfall."

In all the excitement Deetra had failed to notice that the sun was dipping behind the mountains. She had grown accustomed to the perpetual light of the inbetween worlds. Now as she hurried along with the others she noticed the tall trees which lined the roadway, the wildflowers and the ever-deepening shadows that the coming of night was spreading over them.

They arrived at the little house past sunset. It was tucked into the foliage off the side of the road. Ian was the first to approach the door and as he did so it opened. A friendly young woman greeted them.

"Welcome," she said, stepping aside to let them enter. "You are all welcome here."

Deetra looked at the girl. It was Ursula the simpleminded one. She smiled at Deetra, slightly curtseying and motioned her to enter. "You are welcome here, so very welcome," she said again. Deetra was embarrassed. She followed her father inside and sat between him and Curtser on the dirt floor. Ian asked the girl for some tea and then joined the others.

They waited. Finally Ursula returned, carrying a pot of tea and cups for each of them. She carefully filled each cup and passed them around. Then she sat down amid the circle.

"The Prince had made no marks," she said to Ian. "No one has seen him, only rumours."

Deetra watched the girl in amazement. The simpleminded one did not seem so simple now. Her keen dark eyes were locked in official fashion as she spoke to Ian.

"Tell us the rumours," Ian asked, sipping his tea.

"Some say they have seen Rian the orphan wandering about in a daze, showing a pebble to the people that he calls a crystal. But it is a pebble and not a crystal." The girl hesitated, looking about at the others.

"What else?" Ian asked, now turning the cup slowly between his hands.

"That the Prince has him under a spell," Ursula said.

"And how do they know of the Prince?" Ian asked.

"The crystal bearers know. We have seen him," Ursula said.

Deetra stared at the girl in amazement. Ursula said 'we'. She has a crystal.

"How many crystal bearers are there?" Curtser asked Ian.

"There's no way of knowing, but there are many," Ian said, seeing the surprise on Deetra's face. "Many have had crystals in their life and through misuse or abuse, the crystals have lost their power."

"I have never had a crystal," Curtser said humbly.

"Your mission does not require one. You have the jewel," Ian said.

It did not surprise Deetra that Ian knew of the Prince's jewel but there was something strange and peculiar in Ian's manner of speaking. He was not himself. Ursula was not herself either. She was not the meek simple-minded girl who wandered about the village. Something was odd, and the more Deetra became aware of it, the more she noticed a familiar chill rising in her body. She thought of Olivia. Quickly she reached into the pouch beneath her apron and drew out the crystal, holding it up to the candlelight. Ursula wavered and crawled to her knees. "In the name of Hanta the Silent One," Deetra said loudly, "be gone!"

There was a sudden shimmering in Ursula's form. Deetra felt the girl struggle against it, fighting the crystal. Then she was gone. Ian was gone. Her father Starn was gone. She was there in the little house alone with Curtser.

What had happened?

Curtser jumped to his feet. "What? What?" he shouted.

Deetra was too overcome to speak. She had touched Ian; felt the warmth of his flesh. He had felt real. Her father! He had disappeared as well. Then she remembered that along the path her father had left them for a few moments and when he returned, he had returned with Ian. Only it wasn't Ian after all, and the man with Ian was not Starn her father. There were all illusions.

Why?

"The Pink Prince," Curtser said, looking down to where Deetra sat. "He wants the pink jewel."

"And he's mocking up illusion to get it . . . and us," she added.

"But you have the crystal," Curtser said. "As long as you have that we needn't fear."

"Yes," Deetra said absently, holding the crystal tightly in her hand. Then she carefully put it away in her pouch. "But something has happened to my father."

"We'd better go look for him," Curtser said, preparing to leave.

"No, not until morning. On Moonwalk there are no night shadows to add to the illusion, but here . . . " she stopped, lost in a maze of thought. "We'd better wait," she said again.

★　★　★

Morning came slowly. Neither Deetra nor Curtser were able to sleep for any length of time. Often each awoke in the still of the night, checking the room for intruders. Curtser was particularly anxious. He held the pink jewel. Although he was uncertain of how to use its power, he knew now that the Prince meant to reclaim it. But why? The Lord of Illusion was beyond the use of tools. He didn't need it to conquer the village. Rian was already under his power, and perhaps Starn, the simple-minded girl Ursula, and even Ian. No, not Ian. Ian would not fall into the Prince's traps, or could he?

Gently he touched Deetra. She was awake instantly. "We must contact Ian," Curtser said softly. "Call him in the crystal."

Deetra already had it from her pouch, clenched tightly between her hands when he asked. It seemed alive with light, humming at the moment she uncovered it.

"Call him now," Curtser said again. "I must learn how to use the pink jewel."

"But you were told by Sarpent to discover that for yourself," she said.

"But we are in danger; many are in danger," he demanded.

She nodded. Deetra wanted to be with Ian now more than ever, but she was also afraid, remembering how Ian had appeared so real on the road last night.

"The crystal will not lie," Curtser said as if reading her thoughts. "I would call him myself if the crystal were mine." The words caught in Curtser's throat. For a long moment he stared at the crystal in Deetra's hand. Then, quickly he snatched it from her.

Deetra gasped in disbelief.

"Now we will see," Curtser said, rising to his feet. He held it up as he had seen Deetra do many times. Nothing happened. There was no light.

Dawn was coming into the cottage window and he went over and held the crystal to it. There was nothing—no light, no sound—nothing. The crystal was no longer clear as a crystal should be. It was stone—a mere pebble.

"What have you done?" Deetra cried, rushing to him.

Curtser gave her the pebble and turned away. He felt ashamed, unbearably so and the humility of the realization that he could not hold a crystal enraged him. He turned back angrily to Deetra. When he spoke it was not telepathically, but aloud and angry. "It's all a trick," he shouted. "Everything has been a trick on us. Don't you see we have been used by the Silent One. We are fools! There is no truth about anything that has happened to us. There is no Moonwalk, no city of light, no Awakening Day!"

Deetra could not believe her ears. Curtser's rage thundered about the room and the sound of it was deafening.

"Stop! Stop it!" she called telepathically. "You don't know what you're saying. What about the Prince and what happened here last night?"

But in his rage Curtser didn't hear her, and the fact that he believed she did not speak enraged him even more. "You are mad Deetra if you think I will be deceived any longer. I'm leaving now . . . going home. You may stay here if you wish."

Unable to communicate with him, Deetra lowered her eyes. When she looked up again she saw the door closing. Curtser had gone.

In all her life Deetra had never felt so alone. Over and over again she asked herself what had happened. One moment Curtser had wanted to speak with Ian and the next he called everything Ian had taught them a lie. Did it mean so much that he had not been given a crystal? Had he not been given an equally great tool—the Prince's jewel. She shuddered to think of it yet the Elders had placed great importance on it. They had said that it possessed the power of creation. They had also said that he must discover how to use the power. Now he was gone, forgetting that he even had the jewel and disbelieving everything they had come to know as truth together. What would become of him now? What would become of her? She curled up on the cold dirt floor and wept, releasing, abandoning herself completely to the sorrow which arose from the depth of her. Then she stopped. The tension was gone. Gradually, as a feeling of new life began to pulse through her, she became aware of the crystal within her clenched hand. She opened it. The crystal! The light had returned again and the sound of it hummning filed her with joy.

"Ian . . . Ian!" she called into the crystal.

Instantly Ian appeared.

He was solid, flesh and blood, smiling warmly and lovingly, and in his outstretched hand he held a brilliantly lit crystal to prove who he was. "You have passed the test," Ian said.

Deetra sighed, relieved of some great burden. She hadn't known she was being tested, but she recognized the relief of having a weight lifted from her.

"Although you are well on your way to the city of light, you are not there yet," Ian said. "Do you still wish to continue?"

Tears filled Deetra's eyes. She thought of how easy life used to seem as one of her father's household; how she did her chores and played in the fields without a care in the world. Or did she? Her work and her play were always aimed at discovery; at trying to understand life. She was always wondering about something. That was how she came by the crystal.

Deetra laughed, remembering.

Ian laughed as well. He knew her thoughts.

"Where do we go from here?" she asked.

"Where would you like to go?" he asked.

She laughed again and Ian joined her. "To the city of light," she said finally.

Ian smiled, but there was a seriousness to his smile. "All right, but first there are those in the village who may require assistance," he said.

"From the Prince," she added.

Ian nodded.

"First my father," she said.

"A good choice."

"Where do I begin?"

"Well, logic does have its place," Ian said lightly. "Why not begin where you last saw him on the road."

"Will you come with me?" she asked.

"It is my wish to be near you."

Deetra caught the pale blue light in his eyes. There was something there that was beyond divine love; something personal and warm, the gaze of a lover.

"But I wish you to be near me as an equal in spirit," Ian said gently. "It is the only way we may have a lasting and fruitful bond. To do this you must reach the city of light on your own."

Deetra looked deeply into Ian. She loved him as soul and as a man. She supposed that she had always loved him from the first moment they had met in the marketplace. And she wanted to reach the city of light to be his spiritual equal, but more than that, she knew she had to reach it for herself.

A thin but loving smile passed Ian's lips. He had heard the voice of her heart and was glad. "Don't be hesitant to call on the Silent One for strength and guidance," he said. "And now we must part." As he said these last words, Ian stood up, tucked his crystal into his robe and was gone.

CHAPTER 5

Deetra looked up and down the road. No one was about. She rounded the bend where she had last seen her father and paused, assessing the ground on either side of the road for clues. At first there seemed to be nothing to guide her, and then she noticed a bit of cloth entangled in a bush. She picked it off and smoothed it between her fingers, studying it, recalling the clothing her father had worn. She felt certain it matched his shirt. She withdrew the crystal and called to him. There was no reply. She called again. Nothing. She started into the bush beyond where she had found the cloth. Something within seemed to hold her back. She hesitated, looking about but saw nothing. Then from somewhere up the road she heard someone singing. She listened. It was coming from within the crystal, not her crystal but another. The song was not a song and yet it was—a deeply rich humming sound. It was the hum of the crystal and she was hearing it in a way she had never heard it. Turning about, she moved back onto the road and started towards it. She moved steadily for some distance and then the song stopped. She stopped, waiting. She heard it again, this time off to the right, and she hurried off the road towards it.

The thick bush seemed to part as she passed. She hurried, only semi-conscious of where she was going, following the sound. On and on she went, climbing over rock and rough terrain and then it stopped again. She stopped. Just ahead was her father's house. She ran to it.

The door was open.

Inside her father was lying atop his sleeping rug on the floor. He was badly beaten, his face bruised and bleeding. He opened his eyes as though he expected her there.

"Are you all right?" she asked him.

He nodded slightly.

"Who did this to you?"

"My own stubbornness," he said telepathically.

"I don't understand."

"Instead of allowing the negative forces to flow through me, I resisted."

"What were these negative forces?" she asked.

"Psychic forces. The Prince wanted to manipulate me; to use me against you."

"But you were right to resist," she said sympathetically.

"No, my daughter. There is much you do not understand. There are ways of handling difficulties so that you do not get hurt."

"Tell me."

"If a tree resisted the strength of the wind, it would snap. I resisted, whereas if I had relaxed, the attacks of the Prince would have flowed through me and I would have been unharmed. As it is I am injured by my own resistance."

"For me." Deetra said lovingly.

"Look deeper, my daughter. In my love for you, I reacted to save you. But I reacted with passion of mind—anger, pride, vanity. That is why my resistance backfired."

"You will be all right?" she asked.

"Yes."

"Then rest," she said, "I'll watch over you."

"No. I'll catch up with you when I am able. But you must go. There is much for you to do. Remember to focus your attention on the Silent One in all that you do." Starn closed his eyes.

Deetra wanted to continue their communication; to tell her father what had happened in his disappearance; to be comforted as a child again, but she knew it was not to be so. Already his expression showed him to be drifting some where in sleep. She must let him rest, yet she didn't know where to go next. She waited, studying the injury on her father's face and recalling his words as to how he had acquired it. Gradually, an idea took form. What if she were to seek out the Prince; to meet him face-to-face without fear and without resistance. She shuddered at the thought, dismissing it. If the Prince were to seek her out it would be one thing, but she was not about to seek him. Then it occurred to her that the illusions she had encountered—her father, Ian, Curtser—were a result of the Prince confronting her. He seemed to be constantly confronting her, challenging her, only it took her awhile to catch on to the fact that she was being challenged.

What was happening now? Again she assessed the situation. She was in her father's house, sitting on the floor, waiting for some inspiration as to what to do next. It seemed to be a choice between Rian and Curtser. They were her travelling companions. Ian had said that they would learn together; but what would they learn? Deetra was not all too sure she wanted to find out and yet she knew she must. She must discipline herself to continue on the journey.

Cautiously, she reached into her pouch for the crystal and held it up to the light. "Give me strength Oh Silent One," she asked softly as the light began glowing from the crystal. She waited for the hum and then called out to Rian.

Gradually a thin form came to her vision. It was Rian's form. The young boy was sitting on a log surrounded by a small group of villagers who were seated on the ground about him. He was saying something, not through the crystal but audibly and the villagers were answering him. The law of silence was broken.

Deetra heard Rian speak.

"When you feel for something, you have desire for the 'it' of it. The desire sets in motion the very substance of life we call air. To hold desire without disbelief performs creation, continuing the motion set into being. Thus, the 'it' of it comes to pass."

Deetra listened in amazement. Undoubtedly, Rian was quoting from the scriptures he had been taught as a child. Why was he telling the villagers these things, breaking the law of silence, and what prompted him to remember the scripture?

Starn moaned next to her on the floor.

Deetra turned her attention to her father and the light in the crystal faded.

"You must seek the Askan," Starn said softly, opening his eyes. "Only they can show you the power of polarity in creation." He closed his eyes again as if drifting back to sleep.

Had her father heard Rian through the crystal?

There was a long deafening silence in which Deetra did not know what to think. The expression on her father's face showed a great distance between them. He was somewhere in the far world of dreams, not at peace but still, deathly still. The texture of his skin was pale and limp as though he had vacated his body.

She touched his chest. A slow gentle throb reminded

her that he had not died and she felt relieved, loving him, wondering in what strange dream he was wandering. Looking at him she had an idea. Perhaps she could see into his journey through the crystal. She held the shiny stone just above his face and waited. There in its light she saw herself standing next to him, two transparent luminous beings in a globe of light. She was with him in his dream.

Then she saw something else. Off in the distance was a huge dark cloud, blacker than any cloud she had ever seen. It had an opening in the bottom of it and in the opening was a gigantic face twisted in laughter. It was the Prince's face. A cold chill rang through her. "In the name of Hanta, be gone," she shouted.

Starn opened his eyes and sat up on his bed, looking directly at his daughter.

Deetra reached for him, hugging him gently, kissing him on the cheek.

Starn saw the crystal in her hand and watched as she returned it to her pouch. "Thank you my daughter," he said. "Thank you for your love, and your love's protection."

Something in her father's words had a striking effect. She repeated them to herself: "Thank you for your love and your love's protection. That's it father!"

"What Deetra? What is it?"

"The bond of love," she said, slowly reaching for the meaning that was forming in her.

"Go on."

"The positive side of love asks nothing in return; it gives of itself naturally and willingly. It simply IS. This ISness protects us from the negative, demanding and possessive love of the Prince."

"As you have just protected me in my dream," Starn said, smiling warmly at his daughter.

[77]

"Yes," Deetra said. "Then Hanta, whose name I called for protection, is the positive love and the Prince the negative."

"This is true, my daughter."

"And love—true, positive love is a protective bond and it is the positive force of creation." Deetra was filled with joy at the discovery. How simple. All of life seemed suddenly so simple. Wasn't it the way she had rescued Curtser from his make-believe prison. She had loved him in that positive way, had believed he could free himself. Singing the working song to him had only been a tool, something for him to grab onto. And it fit with the scripture she had heard Rian quoting some moments ago. Had he not spoken of feelings and the power of those feelings? Hadn't the Prince trapped him through feelings? But why was he quoting scripture to the villagers?

Deetra looked to her father and could read the understanding on his face.

"You are now becoming aware of the greatest lesson of all," he said, "the infinite power of love."

"And the next step?" she asked.

"Surrendering to love."

"How is that?"

"Experience teaches us all," Starn said. "It is a lesson we learn over and over again. The more we learn the more subtle the lesson becomes." Starn rose to his feet. "As we learn, we grow together."

Deetra watched her father in amazement. Once a sick and weak man, he was again tall and strong. The bruised features on his face seemed healing before her eyes. She rose to her feet next to him.

"Where will we go from here?" she asked her father.

"Our paths separate again," he said.

"But why?"

"You were led to me for a reason and now that reason exists no more," Starn said.

"Where will you go?" Deetra asked.

"Wherever my heart leads me."

"And what am I to do?"

"The same. Follow the truth in your heart and follow it with love. It will lead you to your destiny."

The old feeling of wanting to be a child again returned to Deetra. She did not wish to leave her father; to adventure into the world of lessons and experiences alone, but she thought of Ian and of the city of light. There was yet what seemed a great distance to travel.

CHAPTER 6

Deetra could not forget the vision of Rian quoting scripture to the villagers. As she walked down the narrow path which led to the main road, she wondered about him. What had prompted Rian's memory of that scripture? Throughout their journey together there had always been some incident, some reason for his recall—the symbol in the cave, the old woman's appearance, Curtser's entrapment. Now he was quoting scripture and breaking the law of silence. It didn't make sense. She hurried her steps, jumping over a dead tree which had fallen over the path and scrambled down an embankment and onto the dirt roadway.

She looked about. She was still some distance from the village, yet it seemed strange that no one else was on the road, either going to or coming from the marketplace. It was always so in the middle of the day. She listened but heard no one. There was not the slightest breeze or the sound of a bird or any other creature. A hush had rolled over the land. She turned toward the village and began to run.

She arrived puffing for breath. Rows of tiny huts stood vacant. Doors were left open as if the occupants had left in a great hurry. She moved from one to the other, peeking inside each as she past.

There was no one. No signs of life anywhere.

Turning about, she looked long and hard in every direction. Then she withdrew the crystal from her pouch and looked wonderingly into it. Thick grey clouds filled her vision. They swirled and danced in chaotic motion. Instantly she thought of her father's dream; the Prince laughing at them from within a black cloud. She looked deeper at the grey mass now within the crystal. There was nothing else, nothing except a feeling, a feeling of fear. The fear was not coming from her but from the clouds. She remained still, allowing herself to feel it, to permit the fear to pass through her. The feeling was like an icy wave overpowering the physical senses. Cautiously she withdrew herself from it again, careful not to allow her own feelings to mix with it.

Deetra put the crystal away and looked about the deserted village. This time she saw something she had not noticed. The ground in and around the huts was covered with a thin layer of grey ash. She studied the pattern of it, encircling each hut and interconnecting between them from door-to-door. She followed the trail to the end of the village where it continued on, making a path through the surrounding meadow and into the forest on the other side. She stopped at the forest's edge and studied the area. Obviously the people of the village had taken that route and yet there was not a single sign, not a footprint nor marking of any kind.

Deetra had never been deep into the forest although she had often played at the edge of it. As a child she enjoyed the meadows, the rich golden fields and the bubbling streams. The forest had always been the edge of her world. It was thick and gloomy, the object of horrifying tales of ghosts and wolves. She had never even been slightly curious about the place. It did not appeal to her in any way and consequently she did not know where the forest stopped or what there was on the other side.

She thought of her father, wishing he would suddenly appear. He had told her he would be following his heart and suggested that she do the same. Deetra wondered now where his heart had led him, and if indeed she had followed her heart or rather some mistaken part of herself. She did not wish to go into the wood. Perhaps some of the people had escaped; perhaps she should have taken the road to the marketplace instead of the village; perhaps she should go there now. As she thought these things, she also thought of Rian and Curtser. They were in trouble and she knew that the way ahead was the path of trouble, and she felt certain it would lead her to them.

She sighed in desperation. The forest was the path of her heart whether she wanted to go into it or not. "Hanta, dear Silent One, please guide me," she pleaded.

She decided not to walk the ashen path the others had followed but to travel as parallel to it as she could and still maintain a safe distance. She didn't know if the grey path itself held some power. The forest on either side of the path was thick. Knarled trees were draped with dry, stringy moss resembling cobwebs reached downward to entangle with the brush growing from the ground. Very little light escaped through the density, giving the trees a sinister appearance. At first Deetra was terrified, then she remembered travelling on the side of the mountain with Ian, Rian and Curtser; how Ian had disappeared and they were caught in the thick brush uncertain of how to get through it. In that moment she had heard the hum of the crystal and had followed it, leading the others to the cave. She withdrew the crystal from her pouch now and held it eye level in front of her. A thin ray of light appeared, reaching out to illuminate a thin strip of the grey forest.

She followed the light, carefully taking each step so that her foot went to the ground in a direct line with it. If she slipped to the left or the right, she stumbled, and so, very quickly she learned with precision this way of walking through the forest. Gradually, she became aware of something else—a voice.

At first Deetra believed the voice to be her own thoughts, then she realized that what she was hearing in her mind had no relationship to her. They were someone else's thoughts and for some reason she was picking up on them.

"I can invent with it. I can destroy with it, but what of the third power." Over and over again the voice said the same thing.

As Deetra listened an image formed and she saw Curtser somewhere in the forest, sitting on a rock wall, studying the jewel of the Pink Prince. She could not see his face directly, but his profile revealed there was no mistaking who it was.

She stumbled, caught her leg sharply against a protruding tree limb. "I must pay attention to myself," she thought, refocusing on the crystal's light. But her concentration was disturbed and she stumbled again. This time she sat down on a giant tree root and rested.

Curtser was an inventor, she mused. The breaking device he had made for his father's mill was ingenious and it had saved lives. And he had also discovered the negative power of the jewel she felt sure, but what of the third? Sarpent had said that it was the neutralizing force. What would that do. Obviously it was the result of combining the positive and negative. As both it would change the nature of both. That's it! It was the power which transmutes, bringing the powers to a balance. But what was the balance? It all seemed so incredible, especially since she wasn't at all sure that the understanding she had just gained came from herself or from Curtser, or from both.

Both!

That was it! She knew it; although uncertain how she knew it.

★ ★ ★

It was some time before Deetra again sat down to rest. Since the incident of intermingling her thoughts with Curtsers' she had the strangest feeling that she was not alone. Peculiar shapes loomed at her through the forest. They were formless, invisible and yet she saw them. Sometimes she thought them to be animals and at other times human. They darted ahead and moved about her on either side of the light from the crystal. Whenever her attention was drawn to them she stumbled so she tried never to look directly at them. Finally she came to the side of a cliff and stopped. She could go no further. The way was blocked. She turned the crystal to the right of her and then to the left and leaned with her back to the cliff. Which way to go?

A torrent of screams broke out around her and fleeting formless shapes danced in a semi-circle. They could not penetrate the crystal's aura but performed with frenzied motions just to the edge of it. She tried to quiet her thoughts, to listen to the screams and to try to make some sense of what she heard.

"We are the light eaters, creatures of the night . . . No one sees us without the crystal's sight."

Deetra narrowed her eyes and looked through the crystal's light directly at the dancing shapes. What she saw was ten, maybe twenty half-human, half-animal figures jumping up and down around her. "What do you want of me?" she called out to them.

"The forest has no light . . . no light," they called back in unison.

"How can I help you?" she asked.

The dancing stopped and for a moment everything went completely still. A little man-shaped being with pointed ears stepped forward. "Since the Prince has come there is no light in the forest. We have no food," he said.

"Rid the Prince . . . Rid the Prince!" the others called in unison.

Deetra stared at the little creatures in amazement. She had never truly believed that such entities existed. They were ghostlike as she had heard as a child but they were not ghosts. In their song, they sang of the crystal.

"Who are you?" she asked.

"We are forest Dales," the strange little man said, "we attend to the needs of the trees, the birds and the animals. We maintain the balance here but now we cannot do our job. We are starving. We exist on light and since the Prince has come there is none in the forest. You have the crystal. You must help us."

"Little Dales I will do what I can," she said, then explained how the Prince had made a grey ashen path into the forest and had led the villagers along it.

"We have seen the path and we have seen the villagers," the Dale spokesman said.

"Where?"

"Just north of here in a glen."

"Will you take me to them?" she asked.

"Yes! Yes!" the little beings shouted. "We will take her! We will take her!"

Deetra waited until the little band set off to the right and then she followed, holding the crystal firmly in front of her.

"This is absurd," she said to no one, talking to herself through the crystal. "Incredible." There was no resem

[*85*]

blance between life as she saw it now and life before she received the crystal. Everything was once so surface, so defined and easily recognizable. It was simple living in a three-dimensional world. Now there were countless other dimensions, one within the other and she was living them all at once. She was dealing with matter both seen and unseen, things and beings that were and weren't at the same time. Perhaps Curtser had been right that there was no truth to any of it; perhaps it was all a lie, a trick; perhaps she was living the illusion and the others were trying to save her from it; or perhaps she was merely asleep, dreaming.

She stopped. It was as though someone was tugging at her.

"Shh! Shh!" the little man with pointed ears was in front of her, motioning with his finger. "You are making so much noise everyone will know we're coming."

Deetra realized her thoughts were being heard by the Dales. "Are the villagers here?" she asked.

"Around the bend. We must not go. You will have to go alone from here," the little man said.

"But I may need your help!"

"No. No. You have the crystal."

"Will you wait here?" she asked.

"Nearby. We will be nearby." The little man motioned to the others and they all ran off in the direction they had come.

Deetra hesitated, uncertain of what awaited her. Then she moved slowly, following the thin ray of light from her crystal around the bend.

Rian was sitting on a log with a circle of villagers seated on the ground about him. It was the same scene Deetra had seen while looking into the crystal at her father's house. Could it be? Rian was talking.

Deetra listened, staying as far to the right of the little

gathering as she could and still hear. He was saying something about creation, possibly the same words she had heard him say earlier.

"And that is why the Pink Prince has come," she heard him say in conclusion. Then Rian rose to his feet and walked towards her.

He had seen her.

Deetra held the crystal firmly in front of her.

"Thank you for coming," Rian said. "The Dales promised they would bring you."

Deetra was too astonished to speak. She lowered her eyes and looked through the crystal at Rian. It was Rian but there was something strange about him. Wrapped about his countenance was a thin pink fiber, a web of sorts, wrapping him from head to toe.

"Are you all right?" she asked finally, still studying the boy.

"Oh yes, but I have missed you. That is why I asked for you to be brought here," Rian said.

"Why are you here?" Deetra asked, keeping the crystal between them.

"It is necessary for us to stay until the ceremony is complete," he said.

"You mean, Awakening Day?"

Rian flinched. "We do not call it that here. For us it is Judgment Day."

"The Askans are not judges," Deetra said.

"Nor do they exist,," Rian said.

"And what of Hanta? Can you say that he does not exist either? You have a crystal Rian. You can prove his existence to yourself."

For a moment the thin fibers encircling Rian seemed to slip in their grip and sag. Then they tightened again. "I have no crystal," he said, reaching into his pocket. "I have a little round pebble and you may have it if you like."

[*87*]

He handed it to Deetra.

It was lifeless, a mere pebble, but she accepted it and put it into her pouch.

"How is it that you recall the scriptures to the villagers?" Deetra asked.

"They are the properties of the Prince and I am in his service," Rian said.

There was some commotion a short distance away and Deetra wondered what it was. Yet she knew that to remove her attention from the crystal between she and Rian at this time could be dangerous.

"Look! Look over there! It's Curtser!" Rian yelled.

Deetra turned her head momentarily. Curtser was not there. It was a trick. Turning back to Rian she saw what had been done.

A thin pink web had started to grow about her arm just above her hand where she held the crystal. A peculiar tingling feeling began to settle there.

Rian smiled. "You see, it doesn't hurt. The Prince is really quite loving and gentle. When he finally wraps himself completely around you, you will feel very secure and very happy."

It was growing on her arm. Deetra wanted to shake it off but to do so would mean yielding her attention from the crystal and she could not chance it. The web grew rapidly, spiraling about her arm and reaching up to her shoulder. Was she trapped?

No. The answer came from within herself. Only a person's feelings could trap them. She would not feel now. She didn't have to because the web was only illusion. It did not exist and she would not allow her feelings to tell her otherwise. "Hanta! Hanta!" she called out through the crystal. "If ever you were to share your strength, share it with me now!"

The web loosened and fell off.

Then turning her full attention to Rian, she pleaded with him to call out to the Hanta and free himself.

"No," Rian cried. "You don't understand. I love the Prince. He is like a father to me. I want you to love him too."

"He is the Lord of Illusion and he does his job well," Deetra said. "I respect his talents and his task but I will not be controlled by him. It is not right for anyone to be controlled by any force. We are free spirits destined to learn and awaken. If our freedom is taken away we cannot accomplish that."

Deetra watched the change on Rian's face. He stared at her in amazement, then pity, then sorrow. Tears fell from his eyes as he looked at her, pleading for understanding. Then it occurred to her that although he spoke aloud, she had been speaking to him through the crystal. He had heard her; had carried on a conversation with her and yet the crystal he had handed her had been without life.

She had an idea.

"I've brought you something," she said earnestly. Before I give it to you however, there is something I'd like you to know. When we first began our travels to the city of light I discovered that we had a mutual friend and that we were also destined to become great friends."

"What mutual friend?" Rian asked, brushing a tear from his cheek.

"The gift I bring you is one of love from that friend," Deetra said.

"Do let me have it," Rian said.

"I promised to give it to you when we were alone," Deetra answered.

"But there is no one near us now."

"But we are not alone."

"I can't leave here now."

[89]

"Later perhaps," Deetra said, "I must go."

"But you cannot leave without giving me my gift."

"I'm going to look for Curtser. Perhaps you can join me later."

"Where?"

Deetra pointed to the bend in the cliff wall where she had entered. "Follow the cliff you'll find me."

"But the Prince has made trails for us to walk upon. We were told not to leave the path."

"Curtser is in danger. We must help him" Deetra said.

Rian nodded. "I will meet you later," he said. Then he hurried off to join the villagers and the commotion on the other side of the camp.

Deetra left.

A plan was forming in her mind. Up until this point she had been meeting Rian with pleas. Now she would meet him with action, fight fire with fire, although she was still uncertain how she would carry her plan out. She looked about hoping to see the Dales and called out to them through the crystal.

The little man with pointed ears appeared. The others stood behind him.

"Do you really want to rid the Prince or are you just trying to work for both sides?" Deetra asked him.

"Work both sides yes . . . to rid the Prince," the little man said.

"Rid the Prince! Rid the Prince," the Dales called out behind him.

"All right then," Deetra said, "then you must be prepared to help me."

"We will. We will," they called out in unison.

"What do you want us to do?" the spokesman asked, his ears tilted back skeptically.

Deetra was amused but quickly let the feeling pass.

"I'm not sure just yet but I'm working on a plan. You must be prepared to come when I need you."

The little man nodded.

"Rian is going to meet me in the forest. You will have to make sure he finds me."

"We will. We will!" the Dales called out.

"And one other thing," Deetra said, "Curtser is somewhere in the forest. I saw him through the crystal sitting on a rock ledge. Will you find him for me?"

"We will. Will!" the Dales said again. They started to run off.

"Wait!" Deetra called after them.

The Dales stopped to listen.

"I want you to seek out all the crystal bearers in this forest, even if like Rian their crystal has turned to stone. Find out who they are and gather them together if you can."

"Where gather?" the spokesman asked.

"You know the forest. You decide where to gather them."

"We will. We will!" the little band of Dales shouted excitedly. Then they all danced off in a frenzy together.

There was nothing for Deetra to do now but to wait. Her mind was racing, trying to figure out a plan and she tried to quiet it. There was no plan really, just an idea. The plan was to unfold itself in its right time. She had only to be ready; to be tuned in to what action she was to take when it was time for action. She thought of Hanta, the beautiful glow of love he radiated; how his countenance seemed old one minute and young the next; how he spoke without speaking as she had learned to do. The secret of silent communication seemed merely to be aware of oneself as a multi-dimensional being and to perform likewise. Rian was speaking aloud in his communications but he had heard her every silent word. He was not transmitting in a multi-dimensional way but he was receiving. And Rian had wanted her near him; wanted her presence not just as a conquest for the Prince but more for a genuine feeling he had for her. And he wanted the gift of love from a mutual friend which she had promised. Rian was expressing feeling to her. The Prince had trapped him by his feeling nature; now Deetra would have to do the same in order to free him.

The forest seemed deathly quiet. Nothing stirred. She could feel the cold, hard earth of the cliff beneath her back. She thought of Hanta again; how he had shown her the illusion of the inbetween worlds by stepping into the earth and putting his hand through a tree. She laughed to herself, remembering the magic of that place, of Moonwalk. Yet the physical world was filled with illusion too, only more subtle, denser. What of the Dales? Were they physical creatures? Their bodies were not visible without the crystal, yet their subtle presence had been felt by many. That was why the forest was the object of so many ghost stories. Perhaps everyone saw and felt entities of the inbetween worlds only they were not aware that they did so. Was it not awareness or at least a certain desire for awareness that brought the crystal to people? Was it not doubt and mind passion which killed the crystal's light?

A certain sound radiated nearby. Deetra rose to her feet and held up the crystal. The soft hum seemed to sing to her and she tried to listen to its song as well as the approach of someone coming near.

It was Rian.

She smiled lovingly at him, wondering if he could hear the crystal's song. She herself had never heard it make such melody.

"I've heard that Curtser's in the forest not too far

from here," Rian said, slightly puffing. He appeared nervous. "But first, what of the gift you've brought me."

"Did you hear where Curtser was?" Deetra asked, ignoring Rian's anxiousness.

"The Dales told me as I was coming to meet you," Rian said. "They said they found him."

The little man with pointed ears popped into the crystal's vision. "We have found him. We have found him!" he said.

"Will you take us?" Deetra asked.

"But I cannot go," Rian said.

"But you must. You must," the little man said.

"Deetra, you promised me the gift from a friend," Rian said again.

"But it's a gift of love," she said. "It would be only fitting to receive it while performing an act of love."

"But I may be discovered missing," Rian said.

"Love also protects," Deetra said warmly. "We must find Curtser."

Deetra watched as a peculiar change came over Rian's countenance. The pink fiberous strands wrapped about him seemed to contract and the result was that he looked suddenly angry. But the anger wasn't anger really. It was pain. She waited silently, listening to the crystal, humming, singing, envisioning the flow of its song flowing outward to him. Then she saw another transformation take place. Rian relaxed.

"We must go. We must go." the Dale with pointed ears called out. He jumped away from the two humans, beckoning them to follow.

Rian turned and followed the Dale. Deetra went behind him, extending the crystal in front of her, encouraging its song and light to flow outward at Rian's back.

The crystal's song enraptured the journey, enchanting them and enchanting the forest. Deetra could not resist its melody. She began to sing it. The Dale joined her and soon so did Rian. Even the trees, the bushes and the earth they walked upon seemed to respond to it. With each step the journey became light and more joyous. It was as though the Prince no longer existed, nothing existed except the three happy travellers in a suddenly brightened forest. They were not following the crystal's light, but more the sound and it brightened with each step they took. To Deetra, it seemed that the more they moved with the flow, the more they worked with it, the stronger it became. The sound was not just a melody. It was the music of life and the power which sustains it.

CHAPTER 7

Everything seemed to be taking a turn for the better. Deetra marvelled at the positive flow which guided them through the forest. The Dale in the lead knew exactly where he was going, moving swiftly with a great sense of urgency. They moved on and on, then turning between two rock walls. The passage was long and narrow, then widened into an alcove, the open grey sky overhead. Although there was no sun, it was the first in a seemingly long time since Deetra had seen the sky and the openness thrilled her.

The Dale stopped.

Gathered within the alcove were a number of villagers, among them was her father and Curtser. The little Dales jumped nervously about them.

Rian drew back at the sight of the gathering. "Why are the Prince's men here?" he asked.

"Not so," Deetra said. "I asked the Dales to gather the crystal bearers of the village. You recognize my father and Curtser."

Curtser and Starn moved to the front of the gathering. Starn was approaching his daughter when the Dales stopped him.

"Let him pass," Deetra called out to the Dales. She

started toward him and motioned to Rian to follow but Rian remained behind.

"The Prince's men," Rian said again.

Deetra stopped and turned to Rian. "Wait here if you like," she said, and hurried ahead and embraced her father.

"There is trouble," Starn conveyed in the embrace.

Deetra stepped back. Curtser was standing boldly in front of the gathering, his fists resting on his hips. No one moved behind him.

What was happening?

Deetra studied the boy uneasily. She had not prepared herself for what to expect. Curtser's firm stance appeared threatening, but why? She turned to Starn.

"The boy thinks you are here to challenge him," Starn said. "When the Dales found him he was working with the Prince's jewel. They had to trick him and steal the jewel in order to get him to follow. He's here very much against his will."

"Where is the jewel?" Deetra asked.

"The Dales still have it."

Deetra called the Dales to her. "Where is the jewel Curtser held when you found him?" she asked.

The little Dale with pointed ears stepped forward. "We have it."

"We have the Prince's jewel. We have the Prince's jewel," the Dales called out beside him.

"It is Curtser's jewel and you must return it to him," Deetra said.

"No. No. It is the Prince's jewel. We will keep it and bargain with him," the Dale spokesman said.

"But it won't work. Can't you see there is no way to bargain with the Prince. Curtser has learned of its power and he can help us. You must give it back," Deetra demanded.

"No. No." the Dales answered in unison, jumping weirdly in front of her.

"But you are pledged to assist me in ridding the Prince," Deetra said boldly. "Now that we have the crystal bearers it will be so."

"Show us first. Show us first," the Dale spokesman said, his long pointed ears twitched as he spoke.

Rian, who had stood frozen to his spot now tried to run back into the forest. The Dales caught him in the passageway and brought him back.

Deetra could see how terrified Rian was and wanted to console him but she didn't dare. To show sympathy to him now when he was still held by the Prince could prove extremely dangerous for all of them. She could not chance being trapped by her feelings for the boy. Instead she turned to Starn and asked for his advice.

"Let's sit and rest with Rian awhile," he suggested.

Deetra agreed and encouraged Rian to sit with them at the edge of the passage. The Dales looked on.

"I must get back," Rian said nervously.

"But Curtser . . "

"You said he was in danger; that coming with you was an act of love. It appears more like war to me."

Starn looked on silently.

"All right," Deetra agreed, "you may leave, but first I promised you a gift."

"Let's have it," Rian said impatiently.

Rian appeared angry again, or was it pain as the crystal had revealed before. She did not dare to look through the crystal now. Rian would not trust her. He might run away. She held it tightly enclosed in her hand and called on the strength of the Silent One, asking for guidance and wisdom. Then, as if she had suddenly raised the crystal, she heard its song, the same song they had heard while journeying through the forest. She looked at Rian and when she did, it was as though she was seeing him through the crystal. The thin pink fibers wrapped about him were squeezing him unmercifully. She did not know how he could bear the pain.

"Give it to me!" Rian cried out.

Deetra reached into her pouch and with all the love she could find in her heart she withdrew the pebble he had given her and placed it on his outstretched hand.

It lit up!

A dazzling array of color sparkled from Rian's hand. The boy's attention was caught by it. He held it in his palm, watching, a look which turned from fascination to love. He was remembering. Deetra could see the memory of Hanta on his face and in the tiny images of the crystal-like tears which streamed down his cheeks. The pain was lessening and in that moment Deetra saw that the fiber which had been wrapped about him was falling away, dissolving.

Rian was free! He looked to Deetra with gratitude in his eyes.

Starn, who had been watching silently, reached over and embraced the two of them. The song of the crystal passed through one to the other and joined them.

"Danger! Danger!" called the Dales.

Starn, Deetra and Rian bolted to their feet at the same time. They could feel the force around them. Turning about they saw Curtser.

"Where is the pink jewel?" Curtser demanded.

"The Dales have it," Deetra answered. "I asked that they return it to you and they refused, saying they would keep it to bargain with the Prince."

"Give it back," Curtser growled, turning about to where the Dales waited, jumping up and down.

"We cannot. We cannot," they shouted in unison.

Curtser lept forward and tried to catch one of them, but the Dale slipped through his grasp like a shadow.

"Wait," said Starn, "we must collect ourselves. Let us join with the other crystal-bearers first."

"They are not crystal-bearers," Curtser growled, motioning to the gathering of villagers some distance behind him. "They are the Prince's men."

"Not so. Not so," the Dales shouted.

Rian who had stood timidly in the background, now raised his crystal before him and walked toward the villagers, calling out to them through the crystal as he approached.

Deetra watched. It was then that she saw the simpleminded girl Ursula among the gathering. She started to reach for her crystal, then remembered that she had not needed it to see Rian only moments before, and looking she saw the girl exactly as she would have seen her through the crystal.

Ursula had the same thin pink fibers wrapped about her that Rian had had. Everyone of the villagers had the same markings about them, except Curtser. Curtser's rage was not like the anger she had seen in Rian. The cause of it was not pain, nor fear. It was something else.

Rian returned and questioned Curtser. "Were the villagers already here when you arrived?"

"They were here," Curtser said.

"Did they speak to you?"

"No. They have not said a word, except Starn, who greeted me."

"When did you last see the jewel?" Rian asked.

"When the Dales took it from me."

Curtser shifted from foot to foot anxiously, looking first to Deetra, then Starn, then back to Rian again. It was not like Rian to ask such questions.

"Please," Rian said again.

"I was in the forest, sitting on a rock ledge, experimenting with the ways and means of working with the jewel . . " Curtser hesitated.

"In what way?" Rian asked.

"I had learned how to transmit with it and to act as a receiver with it. Deetra saw me and her thoughts added to my own, which brought about the solution of the neutralizing force. It does more than makes things disappear. It transmutes them and changes their nature."

"You had discovered this before the jewel was taken?" Deetra asked.

"Yes. The jewel had created a dagger image on the rock and was resting in it, just as it had been on Moonwalk, when the Dales arrived."

"And the Dales removed it from the dagger?" Deetra asked.

"No. That couldn't be," Rian said.

"But that's what happened," Curtser said.

"No, couldn't be," Rian said again.

"Are you saying I am lying?" Curtser asked.

"No, mistaken."

"What are you talking about?" Curtser asked.

"Only human creations may lift objects of power. It is the only life form with the power to lift power. It's in the scriptures."

Deetra smiled, delighted to have Rian's vast memory of the scriptures among them again. She turned to her father to share her joy, but he was no longer beside her.

Starn was gone.

"Where is my father?" Deetra called out.

They looked about but did not see him. The Dales were seated on the ground, discussing something among themselves and appeared not to have seen Starn slip away.

Deetra did not call out again. She did not want to interfere with any action he had taken. He would be back.

Curtser did not concede that the Dales couldn't have taken the jewel from him, but he did agree that it was possible that they could have tricked him into believing that they had it. What he needed to do now was cooperate with the others in an effort to discover the truth. If the Dales did not have the jewel then it was still in the dagger where he left it.

Deetra shared with him her discovery that learning the power of the crystal, she had become one with it and no longer needed to take it from her pouch to use it. "Perhaps you are able to do the same with the jewel," she suggested to Curtser.

Rian, who had been listening thoughtfully, broke into the conversation: "The scriptures say that in order to use a power you must first become the power itself."

"Is Deetra the power of the crystal?" Curtser asked, disbelieving.

"I don't know," Rian said.

Deetra was embarrassed and lowered her eyes. She didn't mean to imply that she was the power, yet that was what she had said. She reflected back to when they were journeying through the woods—she, Rian and the Dale; how together they followed the crystal's song; how each experience with the crystal brought some new knowledge of it, some new experience, remembering when she had returned Rian's crystal to him that she had seen through the crystal without it. When she raised her eyes again Curtser was staring at her. "Is this true?" he asked.

"There is still much to learn," Deetra said humbly. "I have had to rely on the crystal so very much. The experiences have made me realize much of its power."

"There's your answer," Rian said. "My lessons have

been in a different order, and yours' Curtser have been different again."

"Yet we have all learned," Deetra said.

"If you have such power, then you can help me," Curtser said thoughtfully.

"In what way?" Deetra asked.

"Look to see if the jewel is on the rock ledge where I left it," Curtser said.

Deetra recalled how having only placed her attention on the jewel that the Prince appeared. "I can't," she said.

"Or won't?" Curtser asked.

"The jewel is not my power," Deetra said. "It is yours' Curtser."

"But you could see where it is," Curtser said.

"Enough . . . enough!" the little Dale with pointed ears shouted, jumping between them. "We must rid the Prince! Rid the Prince!"

"Rid the Prince! Rid the Prince!" the other Dales chimed in, encircling them.

"How?" Curtser asked.

"We must free the villagers," Deetra said. "Somehow we must find out their bond with the Prince and break it. Then their crystals will be restored to life again. Their strength will be added to our strength."

"Any bond with the Prince is always the same," Rian said.

"What do you mean?" Curtser asked.

"It's always the feeling element in man which traps him," Rian said. "The scriptures say it and I am living proof."

"If I had the pink jewel," Curtser began, leaving his words unfinished.

"What would you do?" Deetra asked. "If you knew the power would be there."

"But it isn't," Curtser said, annoyed.

"But it is!" Deetra said.

★ ★ ★

The villagers were disgruntled and discontent. There was an anxiety growing more intense among them. They spoke of the Prince, invoking him by chanting his name loudly. The Dales grew anxious, backing further and further away from the gathering. Rian, Deetra and Curtser had turned their attention to them, watching.

Curtser studied the situation from a different viewpoint then Rian and Deetra. He was not a crystal-bearer. He had discovered the Prince's power through the jewel. It troubled him still that he did not have it with him now but Deetra's certainty that the power of it was still with him interested him. He thought of the Prince, the wonderment he had felt the first time he had seen him on Moonwalk, of Olivia and his capture by her via the Prince's power. Olivia was the Prince's instrument, a being of the inbetween worlds. Were beings like her present in the physical worlds, unseen yet present? His entrapment in the illusionary prison had seemed so real. Were the villagers being held in the same way? And what of the Dales? They were not physical world creatures, yet they were not inbetween world creatures either. Although somewhat invisible to human eyes they were also visible. Did the inbetween world beings see the Dales in the same way?

Curtser called the attention of the little Dale with pointed ears and asked him.

"They are here. They are here," the Dale leader said. "Here . . . here . . . here," he said again, motioning in jerky fashion and leaping from spot to spot. "Many of them. Many of them."

Curtser had been right.

"But they cannot harm the Dales," Curtser added.

"They starve us. They starve us. No light . . . no light," the Dale said.

[*103*]

In that instant Curtser imagined that he saw the inbetween world beings as they had been on Moonwalk, their grey-looking countenances gathered about the Prince; how the Prince seemed to feed on their presence as though the inbetween world beings themselves were his food, just as light was food for the Dales.

Both Deetra and Rian read his thoughts as did the Dale.

"Now you see. Now you see," the Dale leader said. "We must rid the Prince . . . rid the Prince."

But how?

A clap of thunder bellowed in the heavens followed by a tremendous crack of lightening. The villagers moaned and fell to their knees. Curtser stepped in front of his friends protectively, his full attention to the display of power just above the villager's heads. The thunder rolled again and the lightening cracked. A roar of laughter seemed to fill it. The Prince was here, aware of all that was happening.

"Illusion comes in the form of stress, born from it and exists with it," Rian said above the thunder. "Sarpent, the Elder of the Great One always reminded me to relax, to avoid the tensions and expectations of others'."

Curtser turned to the boy and studied him, then asked: "Are we witnessing tension?"

"That is what came to mind," Rian said.

Deetra was astonished by what she had heard. Rian was right. As Lord of Illusion, the Prince thrived on stress. It was he who created it, nurtured it and fed on it. Stress was the food he extracted from people.

Curtser spun around at the girl's thoughts. Her realization was now his realization. Stress was the destructive power of the jewel. It was the pull of opposite forces, the coming and going at the same time. It was the prison which once held him and the feeling which once held Rian.

Suddenly Deetra thought of her father, wondering what

had become of him and just as suddenly she saw him as though seeing him through the crystal. The vision broadened and she saw that he was on Moonwalk, surrounded by light and mist, enraptured by a great humming sound. There were others there, encircling him in a globe of light. She could not see the faces of the others nor were they familiar to her. Although she sensed they were communicating, she could not hear what they were saying. Gradually she became aware that over and over again she kept hearing the name ASKAN.

She turned to Rian who had seen her vision through his own crystal.

"The Askan are those who serve Hanta, the Silent One," Rian said. "They carry out his bidding in both the lower and upper worlds and they guide and teach those who are ready."

Deetra remembered how when her father lie ill he had reminded her to seek the Askan; how many times she had heard the name but had never consciously been aware of it; had never had the consciousness to seek them. Her attention returned to her vision again; to her father and to the Askan. She watched and became absorbed by the light, by the mist and by the lovely strange humming sound she grew to recognize as an important calling from the crystal. As she listened and watched, the rapture of the vision enclosed her, a longing filled her, and then suddenly the vision was no longer a vision. She was there in the light and the mist, the strange humming sound all about her.

Her father was not there.

No one was there.

Deetra stood alone as if bathing in the white mist for what seemed an eternity. She did not think of anything nor anyone. She just was—suspended somewhere between time and space, between being and non-being. The humming filled her, caressed her, nurtured her, feeding her. The sound and the light was all there was. She was it and it was her. Gradually, a subtle change took place. The humming became a melody, music of sorts but none like she had ever heard. The mist became less than mist, more brilliant than any light she had ever known. She could no longer tell if she had a body. Then as if from somewhere deep within herself she heard a voice, and the voice asked: "Do you wish to go on?"

"Yes!" she heard herself answer mindlessly.

The light grew more intense, the music more pronounced. The feeling was thrilling, shocking, loving and more—unbearable. Then it stopped.

Standing before her was Hanta the Silent One. He smiled and in his smile was all the brilliance she had just experienced. When he spoke it was like the music she just heard. "You have come a long way Deetra, but longer is the way still ahead of you. There is no end to the lengths you must travel. Only now you travel knowing who you are—Soul.

"Mind is as body, matter. It thinks in response to the proddings of Soul. Mind is a machine, a mechanism, an instrument for Soul in the physical world. For many lives it has functioned unconsciously, reacting to stimuli from past bodily experiences. Years of automatic reactions have formed aberrations, fears and habits. But now it knows itself. As Soul is now in control, it has the task of mind cleaning. It will take time and discipline and constant testing. But the labor of the task is a labor of love, joyous and exciting. Out of your effort you will gain understanding and a deep love for all life. Your instincts and your feelings will serve to express rather than to control. Each day you will grow more free. Your freedom will create a longing for similar freedom by those who come in contact with you. Thus you are a channel for the divine force."

The Hanta stopped speaking, reached out his arms and embraced her. A surge of love rushed through her and when she opened her eyes she saw she was back in the rock alcove with Rian, Curtser and the villagers.

Rian was sitting beside her. His eyes were glassy and full. "To think that I would have missed such a vision," he said. "Oh Deetra, I love the Hanta so. When he gave me the crystal, he turned his head away from me at the same time. I felt so rejected. Now I think I understand why."

Rian had watched her experience through the crystal.

"I was being tested," Rian said again. "All my life I have felt so rejected, so unloved."

Deetra lightly touched his arm. "That's over now," she said.

"Not quite. When the Silent One looks me in the eye then I will know," he said. "Meanwhile I am grateful to witness another's good fortune."

"It will happen," Deetra said. Then rising, she looked about.

"Curtser!" she exclaimed.

Rian rose to his feet and stood next to her.

The villagers were prostrated on the ground and Curtser was standing in front of them. They were bowing to him. They were showing him adoration.

"What's he doing?" Rian asked.

Deetra said nothing, watching Curtser. He waved his arms wildly over their heads then drew a long straight line in the air, followed by a reverse circular motion. Some of the villagers fell over sideways.

"What's he doing?" Rian asked again.

"He's exercising the power of the jewel," Deetra answered, "although I'm not quite sure what he is accomplishing."

"Shall we ask him?"

"No. Let's wait and watch."

[*107*]

Curtser performed the same motions again and again until all the villagers fell over, then he turned to Deetra and Rian and motioned them to him.

The villagers were lifeless like fallen trees.

"What have you done?" Rian asked nervously.

Deetra stared at the older boy, waiting for some explanation.

"You told me I could work the power of the jewel without having it in my possession," Curtser said proudly.

"You don't have it?" Rian asked.

"No. The Dales still have it."

"And where are they now?"

"I don't know," Curtser said, looking about, but seeing nothing.

"It seems they have gone," Deetra said. "Perhaps they've gone back into the forest, to hide while you were wielding the power."

"Perhaps," Curtser said proudly.

"Surely, if they had the jewel in their possession they would not be afraid," Rian said. "The scriptures say that only humans can . . ." Rian stopped short, watching the anger rise in Curtser's face. He clutched his crystal and stepped back. There was a peculiar pink glow to Curtser's countenance and he remembered a bit of scripture he had quoted to Curtser and Deetra earlier. 'To use the power you must first become one with the power.'

Curtser had become the power of the jewel.

"What are your intentions with the villagers?" Deetra asked.

"To use them to assist me to overpower the Prince," Curtser said.

"You believe that possible?"

"Absolutely!"

Curtser appeared angry again. It was then that Deetra noticed that any sudden emotion brought the glow of the pink jewel's power to him. There was no doubt that he had the power but to challenge the Prince would be like a challenge from a student to a master.

"Perhaps," Deetra began, "if we first freed the villagers from their bond with the Prince, with their crystals restored to power there would be no need for your confrontation."

Curtser glared at the girl. She could feel the force of his power rising against her. She relaxed, permitting the energy to flow through. She knew that unless she resisted she could not be hurt.

"And what about our little friend here?" Curtser asked, turning his attention to Rian who began to tremble under the force.

Deetra stepped between them.

Curtser meant them harm. In becoming the power of the jewel, he had become the negative power, opposing them. Deetra imagined a shiney white wall between them. She could not permit the negative power to flow through her now and threaten Rian's safety. He did not yet know how to protect himself. She utilized the wall as a mirror, reflecting Curtser's exertion back upon himself.

A clap of icy thunder shook Curtser's body. It was the negative power reverberating, returning to him, through him. He was stunned but recovered. He drove his power forward again, charging at Deetra, only to be hit with the same force he exerted. This time he did not recouperate entirely. His body shimmered and shook from the tremendous velocity. Suddenly, he disappeared.

Deetra turned to Rian who was trembling behind her. "He will be back," she explained. "He has simply used the power to disappear until he has had a chance to recoup his forces."

It seemed the villagers were in a trance. Gradually, one by one they awakened and mutely sat about in a cluster in the alcove. Deetra with Rian moved among them, trying to interest them, speaking of Moonwalk and Awakening Day. But it was as though the villagers' were unaware of their presence. Deetra thought of her father, how she wished he was with them; how she was first drawn into her vision of the Hanta by seeing him in the white mist, and how when she was transported there he was no longer visible. She mentioned this to Rian.

"But he was with you," Rian said. "I saw him. He was right next to you the entire time."

Then why hadn't Deetra seen him?

Rian had been on the outside looking in, while Deetra had been within the mist, bathing in it. She had become it. She had become Rian's vision, a part of it at least. She asked Rian what else he had seen.

Rian looked thoughtfully into space, remembering. He reported he saw the milk-white mist and within it was Deetra, her father and the Silent One. He had not seen anything else, nor had he heard anything. The entire scene was simply filled with the beautiful light.

A strange notion struck Deetra. Perhaps everything in life was a matter of perspective, of viewpoint. Perhaps what she saw Curtser do to the villagers and how he turned upon them was not what Rian saw.

Rian anticipated her thought.

"The Prince and Curtser have become one," he said. "When I looked at Curtser, I saw the Prince. Now when I look at the villagers, I see Curtser and the Prince both, like shadows."

Yes, it was true. Deetra was amazed that she had not seen the deep shadow encircling the seated villagers before now. It separated them, isolating them as though locked in by an invisible wall. Just as Deetra had set up a protective wall between Rian and Curtser, Curtser had set up a prison to hold the villagers. It was no different than the prison the Prince constructed to entrap him. Deetra remembered how she had sung the working song to Curtser, providing a link for him to free himself. She began to sing the song now, and Rian joined her.

"Oh, a working day is play, is play
when all the farmers blend their hay
and toil not too harsh a day
then oh, a working day is play, is play."

Over and over again they sang the tune.

Nothing happened.

"Is there nothing in the scriptures about illusion and how to deal with it?" Deetra asked Rian.

"Oh yes!" Rian said. "The law of attitudes clearly states that freedom is achieved through the imaginative faculty; that all of life is illusion established by certain attitudes. If the attitude is one of fear then there will be tension."

"But how can we compete with the powers of the Prince?" Deetra asked thoughtfully.

Rian tilted his head backwards as if reaching for a bit of knowledge which had been stored away long ago. "Competition intensifies the tension," he quoted softly.

"Then we cannot compete with the negative powers," Deetra said. "It is tension which holds these people prisoner, and if competition increases tension . . ." She stopped. Her words trailed off unsaid. She looked at Rian and then to the villagers, studying them. "If only they could realize their own importance as crystal bearers."

"That's it! That's the answer!" Rian said.

"Meaning?"

"When you handed me my crystal as a gift of love," Rian said slowly, remembering, "the mission of the Hanta returned to me. There was a great feeling of love and purpose. The memory was so strong—so intensely positive that I was freed from the Prince."

[*111*]

"Freed from the negative force by the positive force," Deetra added.

"Then there's our answer," she said, turning to the villagers. "The crystal has the power to dispel illusion."

They approached the villagers with crystals extended. The villagers did not move, watching. Rays of multi-colored lights danced in the dull, grey air. The sound followed and the hum was long, strong and clear. Nearing, they paused at the shadow which was encircling the gathering and then they stepped inside it. Thunder roared at them and bursts of static electricity crackled everywhere. It seemed that the forces were at war, negative opposing positive. The villagers drew together, clutching each other close to the ground. The impact was dazzling and tremendous. Rian's body shivered and shook under the pressure, yet he did not yield next to Deetra. They stood within the shadow, the atmosphere electrified.

Then suddenly there was a scream, then another and still another until all about them was the chilling exclamations of terror.

Faintly, Deetra heard a voice, a familiar voice. "Back off. Leave the shadow. You are creating terrific stress."

"But we will win," Rian said, answering for her.

Rian had heard the voice as well.

"Quickly, leave the circle of the shadow," the voice said again.

Suddenly Deetra recognized the voice. It was Ian, or was it a trick. She listened inwardly for a clue but Ian did not speak again. Then instinctively, she grabbed Rian by the arm and hurried him out of the circle.

Ian was waiting for them. His body was wrapped in a globe of light as they had seen him on Moonwalk "This is not the way," Ian said.

"But we were winning," Rian said.

"We were trying to free the villagers," Deetra said

childishly. Ian knew what they were doing. She knew too that the forces were at war, competing and out of it became . . .

"Stress," Ian said, completing her thought.

Deetra lowered her eyes. She had recognized the increasing tension within the shadow of the circle, but had not retreated. Why?

"Control is a most difficult state to achieve," Ian said gently. "The knowing of power is dangerous and harmful without control."

"We meant no harm," Rian said.

"Ignorance can still injure," Ian answered. He motioned toward the villagers.

Deetra and Rian turned about to look.

They were gone, except one. Ursula was huddled up against the far rock wall. The others had vanished without a trace. Even the shadow which had encircled them had disappeared.

Ian beckoned to Ursula, calling to her gently.

Ursula lifted her head from the rock, saw Ian and ran childishly to him weeping.

"You will be all right," he said, taking her hands in his.

The girl was instantly calmed.

"You have your crystal," he said to her.

She shook her head.

"Yes," he corrected, "you have it. Look in your apron."

Ursula dug anxiously into her apron pocket and withdrew the crystal. It lit up.

The girl was free.

"Your warlike endeavors were not entirely a waste," Ian said to Deetra and Rian. "Because of Ursula's simplemindedness she is more open than most. The crystal easily won her back."

Ursula smiled, turning her attention to the crystal which sparkled in her hand. Then she walked away from them and sat down nearby to play with it.

Ian asked Rian to stay with the girl until Deetra's return.

"Deetra's leaving?" Rian asked anxiously.

"Only for a short while," Ian said. "Then she will return. There are private matters we must share."

A thrill ran through Deetra. She wanted to lower her eyes but didn't. Ian took her hand and for a long moment stood looking at her, loving her with his eyes.

"May we be alone?" he asked softly.

She nodded, and as she did she felt the globe of white light which encircled him, encircling her.

She was alone with Ian in the circle of white mist, somewhere atop a gigantic mountain. Beneath their feet was not earth but rock, transparent rock, and down through the center of it and about it was the spread of civilization—villages, forests and great bodies of water the likes of which she had never seen. The colors about them were as intense as the colors of the crystal and the sound like the music of all life. It was breathtaking . . . lovely, so beautiful she could not speak.

Ian turned to her and kissed her lightly on the lips. They embraced. Worlds turned inward to embrace worlds. They loved, becoming one, non-being exploding into being. A soft radiance enveloped them and the sounds of the heavens sang gloriously about them.

"I love you Deetra," he whispered.

"And I love you too," she answered.

They did not speak again for a long while. Ian cradled his beloved in his arms. Deetra rested quietly there.

"Where are we?" she asked after awhile.

"Above the worlds of matter in the land of the crystal," he answered. "We are on the mountain of love.

Below," he said, sitting upright and drawing her up with him, "are the worlds of experiences. When one has enough experience in the lower worlds, he can come here at will."

Deetra gazed into the vast worlds below. Everywhere there was light interspersed with shadows and the density seemed to lessen as her eyes trailed up the side of the mountain to where they were. They were sitting on the top of the mountain but there were no trees nor trails leading anywhere. The ground was not ground although it seemed solid enough. Although firm to the touch of her hand, the ground was light. She could see right down through the center of the mountain. It was as though the mountain was the crystal. It was the crystal and they were somewhere on the other side of it.

"Now that you know, you can come here anytime you like," Ian said, gently smiling. "You can come here alone or we can meet here together."

She looked into his eyes and the tenderness she saw there touched her. "My love," she said sweetly. Then after awhile she asked, "Do others come here as well?"

"Yes," was all he said.

Deetra wanted to ask who and when but she didn't. She knew it didn't matter. They were not on Moonwalk or any place like it. The inbetween worlds did not exist here. This was the crystal's world. Those she would happen to meet here had to have achieved the power of the crystal.

"It is time you returned to the others," Ian said.

"And you?"

"I have other work to do."

Deetra did not question him. She understood that he was in service to the Silent One. She still had much to experience and there was still the task of freeing the villagers from the powers of the Prince. She had yet to complete her journey to the city of light.

She looked up.

Ian was watching her tenderly. "Are you ready?" he asked.

Deetra nodded.

"Then goodbye for now, my love," Ian said.

★ ★ ★

Rian and Ursula were waiting patiently near the alcove where Deetra had left them. Ursula was fondling her crystal, looking through it as though enraptured by some private vision. Rian turned his head to Deetra the moment she reappeared. He arose and went to her.

"All has been calm," he said softly, studying the girl for some clue as to her experience. "Ursula is quite a lovely girl with a deep love for the Silent One." He paused, looking wistfully at Deetra. "I suppose your recent experience cannot be shared," he said. "Ian did say you had private matters with him."

"We must be on our way," Deetra said gently but not responding to the boys curiosity.

"Where?" the boy asked.

"To free the villagers," Deetra said.

"But we don't know where they are."

"There is some law in the scriptures about seeking and finding," Deetra suggested.

Rian continued to study Deetra's face for a clue. She appeared changed.

"Every moment in life enriches us," Deetra said, answering the question apparent in the boy's eyes. "What we experience and acquire through attitude sticks with us. You too have changed Rian. You have grown and broadened in many dimensions since we first met on this journey. You are greater and stronger. Your experiences with the Prince continue to serve you well."

Rian lowered his eyes, embarrassed.

"Now what does it say in the scriptures about seeking

and finding?" Deetra asked. "If you can remember it may help us a great deal."

Rian turned on his heels, thoughtfully. "It says . . . " he began slowly, "that once initiative of pursuit has been taken, that which is pursued is found. The lapse of time between the pursuit and the finding depends upon the urgency of the quest."

"Excellent!" Deetra said joyfully. "That means we're almost there."

"Why do you say that?"

"How far away is Awakening Day?" she asked.

"I'm not sure," he said hesitantly. "I've lost track. Besides there's no feeling of urgency towards Awakening Day. The urgency seems more towards thwarting the mischief of the Prince."

"But he is creating mischief because of Awakening Day," she said.

"Is that a life and death matter?" he asked.

"Does it have to be?"

"It would certainly intensify the urgency," he said.

"The Dales . . . the lives of the Dales are in danger," she said. "Remember the Dales said they were starving from lack of light."

"That's true!"

"Then we have great urgency," she said relieved, checking the rise of impatience she felt. She wanted to speed her journey on to the city of light; to finish the task at hand as quickly as possible.

Rian continued to study Deetra carefully. "We must not rush," he said. "We can take action, but to push creates tension."

Deetra nodded and relaxed. She was grateful for Rian's presence of mind, grateful for his friendship and more grateful still that she was not now alone; that he was working with her.

Deetra went calmly to Ursula. "We are going to leave now," she said gently. "There is work to do in the name of the Silent One."

Ursula raised her eyes and stood up next to the older girl. "I am not afraid," she said softly. Then she tucked her crystal into the pocket beneath her apron and smoothed the cloth on the outside as if to check that it was securely put away. "I am ready," she said again.

Deetra led the way back into the forest. Rian and Ursula followed closely behind. None were sure where they were going or where their search would lead them. Deetra moved swiftly in the lead, yet carefully. Inwardly she pictured the Silent One leading her, guiding her from bend to bend through the dense terrain. And she moved without thinking. Her mind, except for the image of the Hanta, seemed blank. There was no question, no discussion nor revelations. She travelled that way for a long while until suddenly she recognized where they were.

She stopped. Rian and Ursula stopped behind her.

Just before them was the narrow grey path the Prince had made to lead the villagers into the forest.

"It's the way," Ursula said, coming up beside Deetra.

"The way to the Prince," Rian added uncomfortably from behind.

Deetra was quiet, allowing the comments of her companions to reverberate in her mind. Then there was a long silence in which no one moved.

Rian was the first to speak. "Are we looking for Curtser, the villagers, or the Prince?"

Deetra reached her hand to Rian and drew him alongside of her. "It seems they are inseparable," she said. "But we are not seeking the Prince, only to free the villagers."

"This is the way," Ursula said again.

"Yes, I suppose it is," Deetra answered, uncertain. She turned to Rian. The boy was trembling.

"It is not the way," Rian insisted.

Deetra studied the boy thoughtfully. Why was it not the way? It was the way she had entered the forest and how she found Rian. What was the difference? She recalled her feelings upon entering the forest. It was the way she knew she was to go. Although frightened, it had been the path her heart had insisted upon travelling.

"And does your heart choose to follow this path now?" Rian asked as if listening to her thoughts.

Deetra was astonished by the question. She looked into the boy's eyes. "No," she answered. "I came to find you and Curtser and to assist the villagers where I could. Curtser has made his choice and now follows his own path. "We can't save him from it."

"And the villagers?" Rian asked.

"I don't know."

"I do," Ursula said. "The villagers were promised wealth by the Prince."

Deetra turned her attention to the girl. "And you?" she asked. "Were you not promised the same thing?"

"I don't care for wealth," Ursula said. "I went because I did not wish to be alone."

Deetra recalled Ursula's presence in the cottage when she and Curtser had been fooled by mocked up images of the girl, Ian and her father. Ian had never explained the incident to her.

"Illusion is easily presented to one who wishes to believe," Rian said. "The scriptures are full of such documentation. And it is how the Prince trapped me. I wanted to believe. You and Curtser have been ripe subjects as well."

[*119*]

The boy was again reading her mind.

What Rian said was true. And now Ursula was free from the circle of the Prince's power, which was Curtser's power as well.

"The scriptures say freedom is a matter of choice," Rian said, "that illusion has a grip to it which can be shattered only by fulfillment. The seed which was planted becomes the cause."

Deetra listened carefully to the scriptures Rian quoted, allowing the words to reverberate again and again in her mind. Again came the realization which had come to her seemingly long ago. The trap and the release were the same. And now Ursula too was free, but in reality she had freed herself; just as Rian had freed himself. She had been merely an instrument.

"We must leave Curtser," Rian said. "Remember on Moonwalk, we agreed that if one decided not to continue on to the city of light the others would go on without him."

Deetra stared at the path before them. What Rian remembered was true. Yet Curtser was their friend. His struggle for power seemed to be holding him and holding the villagers. And what of the Dales who were starving as a result? She tried to listen to the feelings of her heart being pulled two ways. More than life she wished the glory of entering the city of light; of being equal to her beloved Ian and at the same time she knew she could find no happiness if she had not felt she had done all in her power to rescue the people and the Dales? But what could she do?

"This is the way," Ursula said again.

Deetra looked to the simple-minded girl pointing to the path. Then she realized that Ursula was not pointing into the forest toward the Prince but back to the village where the path began.

"We must go," Ursula said urgently. "We must hurry."

Suddenly there was a loud noise in the direction Ursula pointed. It was coming somewhere near the edge of the forest. Without further thought the three of them began running toward it.

CHAPTER 8

The tall, yellow-dry grass was matted down in the center, a clearing like a huge nest. There was no one visible only a grim left-over feeling of something which obviously had taken place there. The threesome paused, studying the area and looking about.

Thin grey clouds seemed to rise from the ground and linger suspended above the circle of tall yellow grass. It was Ursula who first noticed them. Deetra watched as the girl mimicked their floating movement with her hands, following them as they began to merge into clusters at the far end of the clearing.

Rian wandered off to the right, his attention drawn to the ground. He seemed to disappear into the grass, then emerged again, calling telepathically to Deetra and Ursula: "Curtser is here! Curtser is here! He is either dead or seriously injured."

Deetra ran to where Rian was standing.

Ursula waited behind.

Curtser was lying on his back; arms outstretched; his face lean and sunken, lifeless as though his spirit had been jolted from his body by some tremendous force. His form resembled a shell.

Deetra dropped to her knees next to the boy.

[*122*]

What had happened?

As Deetra looked on the lifeless form she received the sudden peculiar sensation that she could see into the mind's memory bank. By looking deeply in the same curious fashion she had learned to look into the crystal she could see and hear what had happened to Curtser at his moment of death. The playback started from the end and worked its way forward. There was the Prince's image in battle with Curtser. The re-enactment of it seemed perpetual. Over and over again she could see the force of Curtser's thrust against the Prince returning to thrust upon himself. Curtser had had the power of the Prince all right, but it was self-annihilating, devastating to anyone or anything but the pure negative power itself.

Curtser's memory contained a space of total blackness as though that was all and then the pictures started floating to her again. She saw the Dales and the villagers, Curtser was with them, mapping a plan of action against the Prince. Then continuing in reverse sequence she saw Curtser talking with the Dales, the villagers in the background—and then only the villagers. It must have been that the Dales came to Curtser with a plan. What happened to them? Where were the Dales now?

Deetra looked up to Rian who was standing next to her. He had seen the vision which she had seen, only from her mind rather than from Curtsers'.

"What would you suggest we do?" Rian asked, looking deeply at the girl.

Deetra did not answer. Something was becoming evident in her mind, some thought or realization was presenting itself and she was trying to grasp it. For an instant she was sure Curtser was trying to communicate with her, and it seemed she saw and heard the Dales as well, although no one was physically present except Rian and Ursula. It was then she noticed images of Rian and Ursula reaching out to her. It was as though the mere mention of their name drew her attention with such force that she could see and communicate with the inner images of her companions. It was the entity within the entity which answered or came to her attention.

Deetra turned and looked toward Ursula who was standing curiously in the center of the clearing of tall grass a short distance away. What was the girl doing? It seemed nothing at first, then Deetra noticed that as soon as she questioned the girl in her mind that the inner image formed to provide the answer. It was the same with Curtser and the Dales. The method had been so all along, yet only now had she become aware of it. And she remembered now how when Awakening Day preparations were first announced by the Elders that silence had become law. The law was imposed to unravel this great secret of the inner worlds.

Rian was looking at Deetra in amazement.

He had read her thoughts.

He too had the realization.

The entity within the entity was self.

Just then Ursula sharply caught Deetra's attention. A short distance away the girl was standing, looking quietly, but within the inner realm she was calling Deetra's attention to the whispy grey clouds which lingered.

Within, Deetra drew Ursula protectively next to her and then directed her attention to the thin grey whispy clouds. Their peculiar countenance gave rise to caution, yet Deetra addressed them firmly.

"Who are you?" Deetra asked.

"Your friends . . . Your friends."

"Friends?"

"Yes! Yes! Your friends . . . Your friends."

The familiar sing-songy reply identified itself.

"If you are the Dales, we shouldn't be seeing you in

[124]

this way," Deetra said. "And why would you be such little grey clouds?"

"We are shrinking. We are shrinking. Can't you see. Can't you see! The Prince is starving us. The Prince is starving us. Soon we will be no more. Soon we will be no more."

The little whisk of cloud dramatically broke itself into three pieces and merged together again. As it lept about, Deetra caught a glimpse of the Dale leader's shadow-like form with his pecular pointed ears.

"Now you know. Now you know!" the Dale leader said.

"Tell us what happened," Rian said.

"Ask him. Ask him," the Dale leader said, dancing in a circle, a cloud formation with the other Dales. They were dancing about a small thick mass which hung in space.

It was Curtser, or Curtser's consciousness.

Deetra studied the mass. What had Curtser learned? Was he free from seeking power; was he ready to move on.

"It's not that I'm seeking power," Curtser said, his communication pulsing as a heart beat in the thick mass. "It's just that I'm caught in the challenge in having power over the power."

"That's ridiculous!" Rian said. "You are not the power Curtser!"

"But I am the power!" Curtser shouted.

"Perhaps you are the power but not the source," Deetra suggested.

Curtser rumbled about in the thick grey mass for some minutes without answering. It was apparent that he knew what Deetra said to be true.

"The Prince is the power and he is also the source of that power. It is his right to be," Deetra said.

"And is it his right to overpower me, the villagers, the

Dales?" Curtser demanded angrily. "Is it his right to murder, to kill the innocent, to cause flood and drout, to cause misery?"

"The Prince is the negative force," Rian said quickly. "In the scriptures it says that the law of polarity has its reign in the lower worlds . . . the negative is always battling the positive, always seeking to upset the balance or the middle way."

"Rian your scriptures are fatalistic. To accept them is to be trapped," Curtser snapped.

"They are not my scriptures," Rian corrected, "they are the scriptures . . . Spiritual Law."

"Wait!" Deetra interrupted. "There is a way, not to defeat the negative force by force, but rather to rise above it."

"How is that? How is that?" the Dale leader asked.

"Yes, how is that?" Curtser asked.

"Remember the Prince's jewel and the power it possessed; how the Elders instructed that you learn to use that power," Deetra began.

"Yes, and what do you think I have been doing?" Curtser asked.

"Learning," Deetra answered, "just as we are all doing now. Please listen. The jewel contains the three powers—the positive, the negative and the neutralizing force. We have known all along that the neutralizing force contained the power we are seeking but we didn't know how to work with it." Deetra paused thoughtfully.

"Do we now?" Curtser demanded.

"Yes," Deetra said, "Yes, we do."

She hesitated.

"Well, on with it!" Curtser demanded.

Deetra remained quiet, gathering herself in the stillness beyond mind. The entity within the entity, her discovery, this grand realization was the key to it all. Now she wondered how to approach; how to approach the entity within. It seemed to elude her, to slip away whenever she reached out to It, yet when she remained still and 'wondering' she was close to It; no, she was It. It was her! The wondering attitude which her mind beheld empowered the entity within. What was the entity?

Deetra looked up and about her.

Rian was studying her in amazement.

Ursula moved curiously back and forth entranced by the motion of the Dales in their whispy form. Her movements were natural, uninhibited by consciousness. She projected the attitude of wonderment which Deetra was realizing, only Ursula was not aware of it. Perhaps in her simple-mindedness, Ursula would never be aware of the entity; but, except when frightened, she was living as It.

Deetra, carefully and consciously maintained a feeling of wonder, and turning to Rian she asked: "Do the scriptures say if the entity thinks?"

"Are you asking about the power?" Curtser asked.

"Shh . . . Shh," murmured the Dales.

Rian lifted his head thoughtfully, once again reaching to recall a repeativeness he had heard long ago. Slowly, he began to quote from memory: "The Being within is called Soul. Soul does not think as mind. Soul perceives. Soul does not feel as emotions. Soul perceives feeling. Soul does not see and hear as the eyes and ears, yet Soul perceives sight and sound. Soul IS.

The Being within was called Soul.

Deetra was struck by the realization. She was astounded that she had not recognized Soul as the entity; how knowing it is; how all powerful in Its perceptions. Yet it had no power at all unless mind was trained to observe an attitude of wonderment. It was the attitude which placed Soul in command.

It was then that Deetra realized something else. A

piercing, thin, but strong high-pitched sound resounded within her inner ear. Whenever she adapted an attitude of wonderment the sound followed. It was lovely, haunting, unlike any sound or music she had ever known. It was the sound of Soul; the voice from within; the voice of her life and of all life; the voice of the creative force. It was the middle path or the neutralizing force. It was the way and the answer to what they were seeking.

"Well, what did you learn?" Curtser demanded, the thick grey mass pulsed the intonations of question.

Deetra glanced at the limp body on the ground a few feet away. "You must return to your body," she said confidentally.

"Are you mad!" the mass pulsed. "In this form I am not confined. I am free without limits in the physical world. That body is a weight. It holds me back to one step at a time."

"Is that so bad?" Ursula asked innocently.

"Simple girl!" Curtser yelled.

"Wait," Deetra said. "Did it occur to you that taking one step at a time is the way to success in the world of matter."

"What do you mean?"

"That we are an idea of the creative force just as every thing else in the world of matter is; that as an idea we are well-matched to function in the rest of matter." Deetra stopped, marvelling at the attitude of wonderment she was able to maintain and the haunting, lonely music within.

"If you go back to your body," Deetra said confidentally, "you will see what I mean."

The thick mass pulsed dramatically for a moment and then shot across the field. Last seen it hovered over Curtser's body, sank slowly into it and disappeared. Gradually there was movement—an arm and then a leg. Curtser sat up.

"What about us? What about us?" the Dales called,

hurrying to where Curtser was rising from the tall golden grass.

Curtser stood up tall and stretched, his arms waving high above his head. "Ask Deetra," he said, moaning to his movements, and brushing the question aside.

"Yes, I will show you what to do," Deetra said thoughtfully. If the neutralizing power came from Soul and Soul was empowered by an attitude of wonderment, the Dales could assume the power as well. "First, let's all gather together," she said, motioning to her friends.

Curtser was the last to join them.

The Dales thin grey clouds settled in the center of the little gathering.

Deetra wondered how she would help the others understand what she had learned and in her wondering the answer came. She instructed Curtser, Rian and Ursula to close their eyes. To the Dales she suggested they imagine that state as best they could. Beneath their closed eyelids they were to see light and in that light they were to see themselves sitting as they were gathered together. Now watching themselves with their imagination, they were to do two things: 1) They were to listen as if they were hearing something, some strange sound and 2) They were to wonder why they were sitting gathered together with their eyes closed looking at each other in their imagination.

Rian immediately prepared himself to follow Deetra's instructions.

Curtser wanted to know if Deetra realized how precious time was to them now.

Ursula agreed with a delighted giggle and said that she already heard the music of bells.

And the Dales assumed a cooperative pose, poised in space about shoulder high amid the circle of others.

Gradually, the gathering fell into contemplation and harmony took place.

While the others focused on the contemplative task

assigned to them, Deetra explored the high piercing sound which trailed in her inwardly and called upon the Hanta for understanding. To do this she coupled the sound with an image of the Hanta, directing to it an attitude of wonderment.

Gradually, impressions came. They were subtle and inward, yet it was the Hanta speaking without words. It was the high-pitched hum of Soul, ever-opening, ever-broadening and the Hanta as the image of It or channeling through It.

The message led Deetra deep within until she was isolated with the Hanta and the sound. The Hanta's countenance was firm but warm and loving as she had previously encountered. What was different about Hanta now was His manner. He treated her more as a co-worker than as an aspirant. She had learned and had awakened to her learning. Now she had a task and He was merely guiding her as to how the task could be carried out.

The thin, high-pitched music sent her on a deeper journey inward. A great rise of sparkling jewels twinkled all about her. They were forms of life not yet manifested. They were the unborn, yet individually they had their link with life, waiting to be drawn into form. They were as Deetra was, sparks of divinity, only without means to be conscious.

The music unfolded other stories as well. Through impressions, Deetra was able to see the villagers and the nature of their entrapment. It was little different than Curtser or the Dales. It was little different from what Rian and Ursula had overcome. It was a clinging to pleasure and comfort of the flesh. It was fear and ego and lust. It was the attitude adopted by these sensations which trapped them. The trap belonged to the negative force. It was the exercised power of the Prince. To be free, to exercise the neutralizing power one need only to relax, to walk discriminately with wonder on the middle road; to feel but not be a slave to feeling and to exercise control over mind, not permitting facsimiles to enslave with passion.

Within the sound Deetra saw an image of her friends contemplating with her, and a feeling of love rushed from her to them. She understood what they were suffering. Only Rian seemed near free from his fear of the Prince, yet Deetra could see that the negative force would test him, confront his freedom and try to rip it away. Rian knew of this test to come, yet he had not acknowledged that he knew. Ursula could live in wonder as long as she was protected. It was not her lifetime to wake up and realize herself. She lived free if she was free and it was not too difficult for her to remain that way since her being did not challenge the negative force.

The Dales were more special than they knew. They were the caretakers of the material world. It was their task to nurture nature—wildlife and forests, and to keep harmony and balance between matter and the natural forces. It seemed however, that they had forgotten their secret and that which they lived to be. The Dales were pure energy and that was why they lived in shadow-like forms which never fully materialized. As pure energy on the physical plane they had the power to direct energy in order to perserve life. As pure energy in the matter worlds they were a balance between the positive and the negative and therefore not subject to the Prince's powers. It was true they required light to live, only they had forgotten their heritage.

Curtser's position was more delicate. It had been assigned to him to discover the nature and use of the Prince's power as a prerequisite to becoming a crystal bearer. Why it was this way was between him and Hanta, and perhaps the Askans.

Deetra's perceptions came to a screeching halt. The

Askans had come forward in her thoughts again but was denied her by some great power. As the image dimmed from her, her world became focused again on what was taking place, and Ursula, Rian and Curtser stretched alert in the little circle.

The Dales were gone.,

Deetra looked about knowingly. They had witnessed Deetra's discovery of their heritage, had understood, and they had left to do whatever it was they were meant to do. They would meet at some time again, Deetra knew. The bond had been established between them.

Rian rose to his feet and reached a hand to Deetra. She accepted it and stood up. Ursula jumped up, standing next to them.

Slowly, as if resigned to some peculiar fate, Curtser rose to his feet. "Well, where do we go from here?" he murmured.

"Where would you like to go?" Deetra asked warmly, not sure what Curtser experienced in their period of contemplation. He seemed slow to move as one defeated.

"I wouldn't have the slightest idea," Curtser said and shrugged.

"Well, I would," Rian said.

Curtser looked at the younger boy, remembering how he had helped Deetra pull him from the clutches of the Prince. He also recalled an image of Rian groveling at the Prince's feet while on the platform with Sarpent and the Elders. Starn had been present.

Deetra caught his thought. "I don't know where my father is," she said. "The last time I saw him was with Hanta and so I am certain he is well."

"I say let's be on to the city of light," Rian said, hurrying the communication along.

"And how do you propose we do that?" Curtser asked.

"I suppose we take up where we left off," Rian said uneasily.

"Sounds reasonable," Deetra said.

"Well, where did we leave off?" Curtser asked. His sudden interest in organizing his friends reminded him of how protective he had felt in the beginning of their journey. Now, watching them decide, he realized why he had felt protective, and he chuckled to himself.

"On Moonwalk?" Rian asked hesitantly, unsure.

"But how do we get back there?" Curtser asked.

Deetra knew but she didn't say.

Rian grew quiet and thoughtful, then suggested: "We could start up the mountain again, the way Ian led us."

"We already did that!" Curtser said. "There's nothing to be gained by starting all over again."

"We could call Ian and ask his advice," Rian suggested again.

"We could," Deetra agreed, but she knew that was not the way. Yet she would like to spend a few moments with Ian just now. A thrill ran through her as she thought of her love and she recognized the nearness of his presence. Quickly she caught herself. "Curtser, what do you think we should do?" she asked.

Curtser straightened. The brave boldness which had served the trio so well early in their journey now returned to the older boy. "I feel we should return to the platform of the Elders," Curtser said confidently. "I believe our answer will be there."

Deetra smiled. It was where she would have chosen to go.

Rian looked to Deetra, then conceded. He took Ursula by the hand and followed Curtser. Deetra took up the rear.

★ ★ ★

The way seemed to lighten. Streaks of golden sunlight shown through the clouds. In certain areas along the way a thin rain fell. The effect was not dimming to the light but dazzling. The droplets of water appeared like beads of silver dripping from the sky. Then a rainbow appeared. Ursula danced through it, skipping and leaping, participating in nature's great performance. Curtser and Rian kept a sharp eye lest the magnificent scene they wandered through be suddenly recognized as an illusion.

But Deetra knew that it was not an illusion. To her, they were journeying through a balance of the positive and negative forces, the light and the dark, the sunshine and the rainfall. They were on the path of the rainbow, the middle path, the path to freedom, the path to the city of light and her heart was exceedingly grateful and joyful.

★ ★ ★

A great many people were gathered about the base of Bell Rock. It was difficult to see over the heads of so many and the platform was not visible.

"Who are these people?" Curtser asked, suddenly turning to his companions with a protective glance.

Those gathered were not the people from their village. First they were greater in number and although they dressed in the same type clothing, the faces were unmistakenly different.

These people were beautiful. Light seemed to radiate from them and walking into their midst had a wonderful calming effect. Even Curtser relaxed although he seemed to fight it a bit. Rian and Ursula were enchanted, and Deetra was filled with wonder.

Who were they?

[*134*]

"Come, we must proceed to the platform," Curtser said, linking hands with Ursula, motioning that the others join hands to follow him through the crowd.

Advancing was effortless. The people stepped back graciously to allow them passage and a moment later they stood before the platform, looking up.

Hanta stood in full radiance in the center. Next to him was Ian. In a half circle just behind was Deetra's father Starn, Sarpent and the Elders, and others they did not recognize. Hanta did not speak but looked upon them with exceeding warmth and love, encircling them in radiant motion without so much as moving a finger. And there was something else, something which Deetra alone seemed to recognize. She did not look to Ian but she could feel the warmth of his love reaching out to her.

It was difficult to tell how long they remained that way. The love of the Hanta seemed to form an overlap in time, and the space between them seemed not to exist. They were One, a whole. His form was their form and they him and yet the influx they were receiving from him was the force which made their union possible. They were suddenly lifted up on a platform of light and merged with the Great One.

"Welcome to the City of Light," the magnificent Being pulsed.

The City of Light. They had reached the City of Light. It was as though inwardly a cork popped free from a bottle. They were free. A sudden rush of music encompassed them. The Hanta was no longer visible. No one nor no thing was visible. The music and the light was all and they were a part of It, the magnificent creative force. They were IT and IT was they.

As suddenly as it came, the light and sound ceased. Absolute stillness. Hanta raised his right arm as though in blessing, then turned and left the platform. Joy raced

[*135*]

through the crowd and the unknown people advanced first to Deetra, then to Rian, Ursula and Curtser and offered their fellowship and congratulations.

It was some time before the crowd dispersed but it didn't seem to disturb anyone. The company of these people was not tiring nor dull. Instead, their acceptance had a sustaining effect. When they had left, Deetra returned her attention to the platform. Ian, her father and the Elders had gone as well. So had those she had not recognized. What were they to do now? What was expected of them?

Deetra looked back to the others.

They were gone too.

What had happened to Curtser, Rian and Ursula?

Had she missed a cue to leave with them?

Had she been left behind for some purpose?

Looking about, her mind raced for explanation, but none came. She called out to her friends, then to her father. There was no answer. The silence was stark silence and in it she heard only the haunting high-pitched sounds of Soul, calling her. Her mind stilled. Her attention drawn to the sound. A deep longing filled her and she turned about, facing the empty platform and spoke to the Hanta where he had been.

The words which formed in her were not words but impressions, coupled by Hanta's radiant form. She communicated with Him and He with her, although she could not be sure there was any separation between the two. In her longing, she told of her willingness to serve, to give her life to the sounds of Soul and to function as a loving channel for It. She also told Hanta of her love for Ian, of their love, of their union and joy at the opportunity of sharing the path together. Most of all, she told of her love for the sound of Soul and for the radiance which accompanied It.

Deetra's heart outflowed with love for some time,

when finally the impressions stopped. A feeling of wonderment followed. She had never felt so clean, so filled, so giving, so receiving.

Suddenly, there was an inpouring. The Hanta showed her on the inner, certain things which would be her lot, her experience in the coming months. Deetra did not dare to analyze what was being shown her, nor try to reduce it to words. The experiences ahead were opportunities to serve but they would also require confrontations which would dangerously challenge and constantly test.

He walked with her down a long deep corridor, passed through a doorway and led her into a world more brilliant than a hundred suns. He showed her her task of radiating a likeness of such brilliance in the outer world among the villagers. She was to live with them but be not of them. Her presence would be as a candle on the water, a silent wayshower, a channel for the Divine Light and Sound. Her reward would be a greater privilege of service and an awareness of that privilege. She was to BE a co-worker with the Divine One. She was to live completely free of social prejudice, unfettered by mind and body. She would acquire an instant ability to be anywhere at any time in the inner realms and in the outer. It would be her responsibility to learn discrimination in participating in appeals for attention both from entities of the physical realms and the inner planes. She would be a beacon of Divine Love, without personal attachments to anyone or anything.

The Hanta paused, stepping back from Deetra.

Deetra's radiant form wavered. She was giving up life to live only as a channel for the Divine. All she had been would have to be put aside. Love for family, friends and most of all Ian would become superimposed with Divine Love. She could not help feeling some pain at the surrender of it all, yet she knew she must. She had to. Divine Love was the goal of all life. It was what she came into life to do. She would Be a channel for the Great Force. The Hanta would always be with her.

"Are you prepared?" the Hanta asked.

"Yes, I am prepared," Deetra answered.

"Then I will leave you to your task," the Hanta said, smiling.

The radiance of His love filled her with a deep longing, something akin to loneliness but it wasn't that. Suddenly a question swelled with her, something she had forgotten to ask.

"Who are the Askan?"

The Hanta acknowledged her question with a twinkle of the eye. The light of the many suns poured forth, radiating response to her. And in the radiance there was no sight, blinding light, and when it dimmed again, the Hanta was gone.

The Hanta was gone but next to her was Ian. The realization of his presence shook her.

Ian put his arm about Deetra's shoulder. "Are you ready my love?" he asked gently.

Ian was more beautiful than Deetra had ever seen him. The love poured from his eyes like it did from Hanta. He loved her, she knew, but she knew that his love did not possess her. It was the gift from the Divine One which they had earned individually and together. The gift to have a partner in life, a friend to share and realize the task of channeling for the Divine Force. She loved him and there was freedom in her love for him.

"Yes, I am ready," she answered with sureness in her voice.

As they left the meeting place, they saw the many who had been gathered with them, the beautiful Beings she had met with Rian, Curtser and Ursula.

"Who are they?" she asked Ian.

"They are our people," Ian answered softly.

Deetra paused to look into the eyes of her loved one. His answer reverberated in her mind. "They are our people," she heard him say once again. "Our people!" In a flash she knew. They were the Askan, and we are of them, all channels for the Divine Force.

"They are returning to their homes in other villages and some to other planes of life. They came here for the Awakening Day Ceremony." Ian looked deeply into his beloved's eyes. In the silence he seemed to communicate with some deep part of her.

Deetra felt the joy of his inner touch. She had made it all the way to Awakening Day. Their timing to return to the gathering place and the knowing to do so had been perfect. But then anytime and anyplace would have been perfect too.

But what of the others?

What of Rian? Curtser? Ursula? Starn?

The answer came just as it was being asked.

They were waiting for her in the village.

THE END, BOOK ONE